REQUIEM FOR BOONE

GENE RODDENBERRY'S
EARTH: FINAL CONFLICT
Novels from Tor Books

The Arrival
by Fred Saberhagen

The First Protector
by James White

Requiem for Boone
by Debra Doyle and James D. Macdonald

Visit the *Earth: Final Conflict* website at
www.efc.com
www.allianceatlantis.com

GENE RODDENBERRY'S

EARTH

FINAL CONFLICT™

REQUIEM FOR BOONE

DEBRA DOYLE AND
JAMES D. MACDONALD

EBURY
PRESS

First published 2000 by Tor® Books
A registered trademark of Tom Doherty Associates, LLC New York, USA

10 9 8 7 6 5 4 3 2 1

First published in the UK in 2000 by Ebury Press
Random House, 20 Vauxhall Bridge Road, London SW1V 2SA

Random House Australia Pty Limited
20 Alfred Street, Milsons Point, Sydney, New South Wales 2061, Australia

Random House New Zealand Limited
18 Poland Road, Glenfield, Auckland 10, New Zealand

Random House South Africa (Pty) Limited
Endulini, 5A Jubilee Road, Parktown 2193, South Africa

The Random House Group Limited Reg. No. 954009

A CIP catalogue record for this book is available from the British Library

Jacket art by Cliff Nielsen
Edited by James Frenkel

ISBN 0 09 187330 4

www.efc.com
www.allianceatlantis.com

www.randomhouse.co.uk

Papers used by Ebury Press are natural, recyclable products made from wood grown in sustainable forests.

Printed and bound in Denmark by Nørhaven A/S, Viborg

For Patrick and Teresa for their kitchen table,
Christina Opalecky for first reading,
and John Klima and Jeffrey Dreyfus
for services above and beyond.

GENE RODDENBERRY'S

EARTH
FINAL CONFLICT™

REQUIEM FOR BOONE

ONE

Out above the ocean, the aircraft swung low, below the clouds, and banked to a new heading—away from the security of UN-controlled territory, and into the hazardous and uncertain north. For Major Will Boone, Army Special Operations, the trip had been long and hard enough already without adding danger to the mix. He was too tall to be a jet jockey—assuming that he would ever have wanted to do something that stupid—and in any case the FA-16 wasn't designed to carry passengers. He'd spent the journey so far crammed into the jump seat behind the pilot, with his knees up around his ears.

The voice of the pilot came over the audio link in Boone's flight helmet. "Stand by. We're about to enter the hot zone."

Not long now, Boone thought. As always, he felt a surge of adrenaline, combined this time with sheer relief at the prospect of finally getting out of his uncomfortable seat.

The heads-up display in the fighter's cockpit showed a trace of color forward—false color, Boone knew, computer generated and projected on the inside surface of the cockpit bubble. With the FA-16 shrieking along at 1.2 times the speed of sound, the symbolic images didn't take long to differentiate. One of the blobs of color morphed into a blue wall beginning a little above the water's surface.

"What's that up ahead?" Boone asked.

"Blue's for sensors," the pilot said. "Things that show up in blue can't hurt us themselves, but they'll get the word out to people who can. That one there's a patrol boat with SUREPAVE radars."

"What's the usual procedure?"

"If we duck down under, we can get detected by Mark 1 Mod 3 eyeballs anyway, plus our fuel efficiency goes straight to hell. So we're going through."

"Your show."

"Damn straight. Countermeasures, stand by, deploy." The pilot turned a switch on the control panel, and the blue wall in the heads-up display faded to perhaps half its previous intensity, becoming a pale-blue mist. The pilot continued talking himself through the checklist. "Stand by, flares. Stand by, execute."

A thump, more felt than heard, sounded from the after part of the FA-16's airframe. A hole of clear air appeared in the center of the misty blue wall, dead ahead of the aircraft.

"Hey diddle diddle, right up the middle." The pilot goosed the throttles to zip through the apparent hole before it closed. "And here we are."

Low and green—true green this time, and not a

projected image—the China coast appeared on the horizon beyond the cockpit bubble. At almost the same time, a host of red shapes popped up in the false color display: inverted cones, bright red at the bottom point and diminishing in intensity as they grew wider; scarlet mushrooms hovering just above the ground; and an assortment of crimson trees, spider-webs, and pillars, all mixed in with more blue sensor images. Where the red images overlapped the blue ones, the color was purple to magenta.

"Party time," the pilot said. He sounded almost happy—more proof, Boone decided, that all zoomies were crazy. "All those red shapes are things that can hurt us."

"What exactly are we looking at?"

"A regular mixed-fruit cocktail. The upside-down cones over there are gun emplacements. Max range at the wide end of the cone, max accuracy at the point. The mushroom shapes are missile launchers. Those are hazardous to your health everywhere inside their lock-on zone, but a good pilot can take you down under the mushroom cap, below the minimum lock-on range."

"And you're a good pilot."

"That's what they tell me."

"What's yellow?" Boone asked, as the pilot slewed around the trunk of a red tree, impossibly high.

"Command and control. Their comms systems. Want to have some fun?"

"I want to carry out my orders," Boone said. He didn't know what a jet jockey might consider "fun" under the circumstances, and he didn't want to find out.

"Understood. Deliver you to CommOps, say adios."

They banked hard right, then left, to slalom around two more red pillars. Abruptly, on the heads-up, a wall appeared dead ahead—a dark red-purple wall, covered with yellow vines. It stretched from horizon to horizon on either side, and rose up from the bottom of the display to vanish out of sight overhead.

"The Great Wall of China, coming up," said the pilot. "Hold on to your ass."

Boone didn't feel an answer was needed. The wall got nearer and nearer. It must be huge, he thought, for the approach to take so long. In the seat ahead, the pilot was talking his way through another checklist.

"Stand by flares. Stand by ACM. Stand by PCM. On four. Three. Two. One. Execute, execute, execute. Afterburner, engage."

Boone felt himself pushed back into his seat as the FA-16's afterburners dumped raw jet fuel into the tailpipe. Then the horizon scrolled up, and Will's stomach hit the back of his throat. The pilot pushed down into a steep dive, trading altitude for speed.

In the heads-up display, orange lines rose from the surface, and white lines streaked down from overhead. Black balls appeared in the matrix of the wall.

"Target zones. Gotta stay out of them," the pilot said, his voice very calm.

He twisted and yawed left, putting the aircraft into a sideslip to ease around something that appeared in the heads-up display as a black cylinder. The unknown object slid below the FA-16's starboard wingtip. Without warning, the black cylinder filled with white light, and the plane shuddered in the grip of a shock wave.

"That white stuff was real," the pilot said. Then, "Dammit."

A black ball had appeared ahead of them in the display. There was no room to turn right or left, no way to climb above the ball or dive below it.

"Missile lock, trace, fire," the pilot chanted, like a man reciting a prayer. A double thump sounded—coming from under the wings this time. Two streaks of light shot away forward, then zoomed up to intercept one of the white lines falling down from above. A moment later, they entered the black ball, and the heads-up display grayed out in every direction. In short order came a blast, a shock, and the unmistakable feeling of metal fragments hitting the airframe.

"Close but no cigar," the pilot said. He was flipping switches, turning new-burning red lights on the control panel back to green. The gray-out vanished.

Then they were out of the black wall, and facing only red mushrooms and inverted cones. The aircraft was still doing a roller-coaster imitation, banking and twisting around the 3-D projections. A red pillar appeared before them as a new weapons system came on line. With a stomach-twisting maneuver, the pilot avoided that threat as well.

Then a new color appeared in the display: a pure emerald green, overlying the mottled gray-green of the natural landscape.

"Friendlies, ahead," the pilot said. "Into the slot, and we're home." He keyed up the recognition routine, and the green began to flash. "They're expecting us."

Then the red markers were all astern, and they were in a green wedge, flying down to an airstrip deep in the Chinese hinterland. The touchdown was fast, smooth, and professional. Once the FA-16 was on the hardstand, its canopy opened. Will and the pilot descended a ladder that the ground crew rolled up. As an aircrewman led them both away, Boone glanced back at the plane. Its port wing had a half-moon shape chewed out of the trailing control surface. That near miss had been pretty near.

* * *

The base itself was nothing special—a huddle of drab-colored prefab buildings inside a chain-link perimeter fence surmounted with barbed wire. Boone had seen a dozen or more like it over the course of his Army career. It existed to service the airstrip, and to house on a temporary basis the men and matériel passing through the base to points farther in-country. Once conflict in the area died down, the whole setup could be dismantled almost overnight, and shipped back to the States as containerized cargo.

At base ops, Boone saluted the officer of the day and presented his orders. The officer of the day looked over the orders, then looked at Boone.

"So you're the SpecOps guy?"

"That's right."

"We were told to expect you. Well, here's the drill. Word is that Dog Company is in trouble, and you're the poor SOB who's going to pull them out."

"A simple extraction?"

"Extraction, yes. Simple—remains to be seen. They were last heard from out past the Kush, no word since."

"How long?"

"Three weeks."

"Three weeks? They could be anywhere by now."

"That's why you're here," the officer said. "You're supposed to be some kind of hot operator. Well then, hotshot, operate."

Boone suppressed a sigh. "Give me as much intel as you've got, then."

"Come to the sitrep briefing at fifteen hundred and you'll get all the intel we have. Meanwhile, we have space for you in the Bachelor Officers' Quarters. Report there, and settle in. You're not going to be going anywhere before tomorrow morning anyhow. Where's your kit?"

"I'm wearing it."

The officer of the day looked dubious. "Bare hands and an Army uniform?"

"Got it."

The last thing that Will Boone heard as he left the operations shack was the officer of the day saying to one of the techs, "More balls than brains," before the door swung to.

* * *

When the briefing came, Will Boone wasn't at it. Nor did the guards at the perimeter, human and electronic, see him go. Boone wasn't above telling a fib or two, even to the duty officer at an advance base who didn't really, when you got down to it, have the need to know. One way to elude pursuit is to disguise the time the chase begins—so when the people who were hanging around waiting to tail Boone got started on surveilling the intel hut and waiting for him to come out, Boone was already twelve hours west, dressed in a safari jacket and carrying a camcorder whose logo identified it as the property of Global News Affiliates.

Boone knew that there was no way that a man with his height and his Western features was going to blend into a predominantly Asian crowd. Instead, he'd made a virtue out of his difference. People would see him, but they wouldn't see Will Boone, Special Ops Major; they'd see a reporter, one of dozens covering the current phase of the Sino-Indian conflict.

In a war fought primarily over the control and context of information, news reporters were valued resources for both sides, and passed freely back and forth. The guy Boone had gotten the camera from hadn't been a GNA employee any more than Boone was, except maybe on paper. Boone suspected that he was a GRU man, from the ex-Soviet Union. A lot of them had gone into private practice when the old USSR came down, selling their expertise to anyone with a checkbook. Not that it mattered—the man had the sign, the countersign, and the goods, and that was enough.

Boone caught a train out of Tengchong, riding in the second-class compartment along with a crowd of other passengers—all the ones who could afford to buy their way out of third class, but who didn't have enough money or clout to get themselves a private compartment up in first. He made himself as comfortable as he could, flanked by an old woman reading a mainland Chinese paper-and-print magazine and a huddle of adolescents in quilted jackets. The teenagers had a handheld game set they were passing back and forth, with much noise and high spirits; the sight of them reminded Boone that it was time to give the folks back in D.C. a status report.

He pulled out his global, the combination cell-vidphone that had made Jonathan Doors the richest man on Earth—surpassing even the titans of past centuries—and made a call. The call was going to a drop address, and the global itself was clean, but the message would reach those who needed to hear it.

"Rover is in," he said, and broke contact. Now the people back home wouldn't worry for a while. The simple message would serve to let them know that he was alive, not under duress, and on task.

He reviewed the mission in his mind. A few days ago, Dog Company, off in old Tibet, had started reporting anomalous data, and then had gone completely dark. Now Boone was supposed to check up on them and, if necessary, to pull their asses out of the fire.

Boone frowned slightly. The base ops guy had known the name of the extraction target. That was bad. The fewer people who knew Boone's business, the better he liked it.

He put his global away and looked out the window. To the north, the sky was blue along a flat horizon; cultivated fields growing some kind of low green crop stretched out as far as the eye could see, dotted by a few structures—very few—situated too far off for him to tell for sure what they were.

The train swayed into a curve. Except for the teenagers, no one talked. The train was full, but the people in it had the dulled expressions of people who had been traveling too long, for reasons that they didn't like.

Boone glanced again toward the north. What was it over there?—*something* out there had drawn his attention, that much he was sure of. He looked closely, trying not to stare. Staring would draw people's attention, and that he didn't want.

There it was. A flash in the sky, like something reflecting the sun. He judged that the flash had about a ten degree elevation above the horizon. He put the dot of bright light into alignment beside a scratch on the window glass, and waited. Whatever the object was, it wasn't moving relative to the train, but it *was* getting larger: something inbound, constant bearing, decreasing range . . .

Missiles, thought Boone. Coming this way.

—text of message sent from Kate Boone to Major William Boone via the United Nations Expeditionary Force Network (UNEF.Net)

Darling —

I saw on the news today that they were fighting in [DELETED BY UNEF.NET SECURITY BOT]. Since I don't know where you are—the only letter I've gotten from you so far had so many security-bot auto-deletes in it, I think it was more holes than text—I'll pretend that you're safe behind the lines in [DELETED BY UNEF.NET SECURITY BOT], drinking sake and reading other people's mission reports.

I know it's going to be weeks and weeks before you get a chance to download this, since I don't think they have secure terminals over there in [DELETED BY UNEF.NET SECURITY BOT]. But I'm going to keep on writing to you just the same. That way you'll have a nice full mailbox waiting for you when you get back to sort-of-civilization.

I started my new job this morning. I don't know for certain what I'm doing there—nobody tells us data wranglers anything anymore—but at least it's closer to home, and the new boss can't possibly be as bad to work for as the Weasel used to be.

Mr. [DELETED BY UNEF.NET SECURITY BOT] definitely isn't a weasel. More like everybody's favorite uncle—except that kindly gray-haired uncles don't have the sort of clout it takes to get their pet project assigned [DELETED BY UNEF.NET SECURITY BOT] data wranglers and a [DELETED BY UNEF.NET SECURITY BOT] full of dedicated hardware in the middle of a shooting war.

So far, I like him, even if he does have more political connections than an octopus has tentacles. He lets people with friends overseas browse the UNEF open data feed during their lunch breaks. The connection at work is [DELETED BY UNEF.NET SECURITY BOT] than anything we can get at home—[DELETED BY UNEF.NET SECURITY BOT] than anything the Weasel ever had, too. I don't know what the project did to rate that kind of a hookup. For all I know, the Octopus has [DELETED BY UNEF.NET SECURITY BOT]'s private phone number and a collection of blackmail photos.

In the meantime, you can amuse yourself by envisioning me wrestling with the Octopus's data. I still don't know where it all comes from. Some of it's government-generated material, I can follow a trail well enough to see that, but a lot of it is private-sector stuff.

Expensive stuff, too. I always thought that [DELETED BY UNEF.NET SECURITY BOT] and [DELETED BY UNEF.NET SECURITY BOT] refused to sell their proprietary data to anyone, period. The Octopus must have a budget big enough to buy half of [DELETED BY UNEF.NET SECURITY BOT]—either that, or he knows where to go for really good freelance data-acquisition.

Anyhow, starting the new job was the high point

of my week so far. First runner-up was buying some more flowers for the yard—the nursery is right on the way home from work. So far, though, it's been raining too hard for me to go outside and plant them, and I think I'm coming down with a cold anyway.

I hope the weather is better over there in [DELETED BY UNEF.NET SECURITY BOT], or wherever you really are.

Love,
Kate

TWO

The incoming missiles were about ten degrees above the horizon. It was hard to tell how far off they were, though, without knowing their exact type and size. Worst case would be glider bombs, the remote-guided explosives used for harassment and interdiction.

Boone decided that worst case would be about right. With a deliberate lack of haste, he stood up and left his seat. He had no desire to start a rush that would hinder his own efforts to get clear.

He edged past the group of teenagers with the handheld gamebox. For a moment he felt guilty about not speaking up to give them a warning, but the cold voice of reason pointed out that a warning, at this point, would accomplish nothing except to cause a panic. The cold voice of reason was a real bastard sometimes.

Boone told himself to forget about the kids, and kept on walking at a brisk pace toward the rear of the train. In the open-bay car, the passageway between the seats was narrow, forcing him to hold his video camera up in front of him to avoid hitting anyone. With the peculiar clarity of mind that sometimes comes from incipient disaster, he found himself noting that some of the seats were upholstered in sturdy cloth, others in cracked blue vinyl.

A real mixed bag of materials, he thought. Thrown together any which way.

Like the passengers. Who are going to die.

He walked a little faster.

Out on the platform of the train he paused and looked at the ground going past. Thirty, maybe forty, miles per hour. Not an impossible jump for a trained man, but still a good way to end up dead or crippled.

He looked over to the north, and searched the sky for a moment, looking for that fatal glint of light, and finding it. There were the glider bombs, closer now: definitely racking in on the train.

Boone wondered how the bombs would strike. Maybe they would hit up forward, at the engine. That would make the lead cars jump the tracks, but the last cars would be safe, the energy of the train's momentum absorbed by the accordioning of the first several cars. Or maybe the first bomb would head to the front of the train, and the second to the rear. One thing was certain—whoever had programmed the missiles for locomotive destruction would know as much as Boone did about how energy gets expended.

Meanwhile, the ground outside the train didn't look any softer than it had a few moments before. A water jump would be safer, if there was water anywhere about . . . Boone stuck his head out into the wind and looked forward. Nope, no likely-looking streams coming up. Not even a mud puddle.

A couple of feet below where he stood, the train's airbrake line ran above the couplers. Only a thin platform of diamond-tread metal separated his boot soles from the machinery linking the cars. If he could cut the brake line, he'd have a better chance of surviving to carry out his mission. Reason enough to try; the fact that he had a slim chance that way of saving a few of the other passengers was incidental.

He took the shoulder strap from his camera. Lying down on the platform, he tried to swing the strap's weighted buckle end underneath the brake line. It took him two tries to snag the line and retrieve the loose end of the strap—too long, he thought. The engineer's undoubtedly seen the bombs already. For all the good that seeing them will do.

He pulled at the ends of the strap and hauled the brake line up within reach of where he lay on the platform. Holding the line in position with one hand, he fished out a small pocketknife with the other. Cutting the lines would be tough, but if he could sever even one of them, the train's air brakes would apply.

He almost had it—the blade of his folding knife was open in his hand—when a roaring explosion came from up near the locomotive, and another one from the rear of the train, and he was jolted forward. His back smashed against the door of the railway car, and the air around him hissed with fire while his ears rang with the explosions.

The train was definitely slowing. The air brakes were cut—by the rocket strikes, Boone knew, and no thanks to his own futile efforts. Without the air to hold them, the brake shoes were applied to the wheels by the great springs.

Boone looked at the ground next to the tracks and decided that the train was going slowly enough after all. He tucked his camera into his arms and jumped, rolling like a paratrooper, letting his momentum soak up into distance traveled rather than into compressing his spine.

Then the jump was over, and he pushed to his feet, looking around. As he'd half expected, the missiles had hit the train at both ends and turned it into a mass of smoking wreckage, with the individual railway cars piled up against each other like thrown sticks. Survivors, bleeding and blackened, were pulling themselves and others out of the broken cars. One of the cars had caught fire, and red flames roared from its shattered windows.

I'm a reporter, Boone thought. Time to look like one.

He raised the camera to his shoulder and started filming. Will Boone had long ago learned the cardinal rule of basic invisibility: Do what everyone expects, and no one notices you. Put a tall westerner at a flood or a train wreck or a burnt-out village, give him a professional-sized vidcam loaded with company logo stickers, and he'll be invisible so long as he's looking through that camera.

In a sudden cloud of dust and smoke, a helicopter with first-aid symbols painted on its side landed near the train, followed by a second helicopter bearing the colors and trademark of Global News Associates.

Boone lowered his vidcam and walked over to the second helicopter.

"Clint Stark, Haiphong bureau," he said to the pilot. "Traveling on assignment. Got some great footage. Give me a lift to the nearest uplink site?"

"Sure, hop in," the pilot roared back at him over the racket of the copter's engine.

A female reporter, looking clean and trim against a background of dazed survivors and twisted rubble, had climbed down out of the helicopter while Boone and the pilot were speaking. Her male companion pointed a camera of his own at her. She talked for a minute or two, with the train still burning in the background, then shouted "Let's go!" and reboarded the helicopter.

Inside the chopper it was too noisy to talk. As the smoking wreckage of the train dwindled to a hazy smear across the sky behind them, Boone finally relaxed enough to start thinking about the best way to get closer to Dog Company, now that travel by train was out. So was any other method of transportation that required him to purchase tickets—whether electronically, or face-to-face at a cash window, it didn't matter. He couldn't afford the visibility.

The attack on the train could have been a random terrorist attack, meant to embarrass the government of mainland China and demonstrate the hazards of travel to its citizenry—but it wasn't very likely. The officer back at the base had known enough about Boone's errand to be waiting for his arrival, and if base security was that lax, any number of interested parties could have gotten hold of the information.

Destroying a whole train in order to stop a single Special Operations major was serious overkill, of course, and most people would dismiss the idea out of hand on that account. "Most people" didn't have a clue about the strategy and tactics of modern information-based warfare, either. Boone wasn't ready to discard the possibility that somebody considered him dangerous enough to be worth an entire passenger train full of lives.

As soon as they reached the city, the helicopter settled down onto the helipad atop a downtown office building and shut off its rotors. The three passengers walked out together—the reporter, her cameraman, and Boone.

"Here," Boone said to the cameraman. He pulled out the tape cartridge from the side of his own camera. "Good footage here, shows you everything. You can use it for your report."

"Have to talk to the talent about that," the cameraman said. "George Murray." He stuck out his hand. "Good to see you. I thought I knew everyone who was out here."

"Clint Stark," Boone said, shaking the proffered hand. "I'm just passing through. Not my beat here. What's going on out west? It's where I'm heading."

"All screwed," Murray said. "Nothing coming out of there."

"Wonderful."

They had reached the stairway from the roof and were two floors down before Boone said, "Where can I get a fresh film cart and some gear? I lost most of everything in the attack."

"Don't say 'attack,'" Murray told him. "That was a 'tragic rail disaster,' and the authorities are convening a safety council meeting right now to determine whether it was human error or mechanical faults that caused the accident."

"Things are like that around here?"

"Like that and worse. If you're planning to tell the truth or any part of it, keep on traveling. This war isn't the place for it."

Boone put the camera down on the floor in the GNA employee lounge and continued out into the street. Clint Stark, GNA reporter, had served his purpose and existed no longer. Boone would have another identity and another mode of transportation lined up in minutes.

Meanwhile, there was a company of soldiers who were looking for a rescue. Boone picked up his pace. He wanted to be well out of town by sunset.

* * *

The last thing that Lieutenant Felipe Menendez had expected to see, up here in the jagged mountains of the Hindu Kush fifteen klicks from the nearest vil, was another UN trooper, especially a Special Operations man from the U. S. of A. Menendez and the rest of Dog Company had, in fact, expended considerable effort over the past few weeks in order to avoid such encounters. With Special Operations, you never could tell in advance whether they'd help you out of trouble, or push you further into it for some reason you didn't have a need to know.

Even in peacetime, or in a good clean war, dealing with SpecOps was a risky business. Up here in the high border regions of India and Pakistan and the fragmented remnants of what had once been Soviet Central Asia, the conflict had turned dirty a long time before. Information viruses and mindworms could piggyback on the most innocuous-seeming data, making high-tech equipment worse than useless. An obviously broken piece of gear might be abandoned, or a malfunctioning one repaired, but one that returned false data undetected could go on telling lies indefinitely. Worse yet, any item of equipment still in good order thereby became suspect, a possible agent of shadowy figures on the other side.

True to form, the man from Special Operations showed up alone and in mufti. Menendez had seen SpecOps guys in uniform a few times, but only on formal occasions and never in the field. This one dressed like an out-of-work surveyor, in hiking boots and corduroy trousers and a heavy down-filled jacket, and he drove a Russian-built Fiat truck with a chassis more rust than paint. He came up along the dirt road from the village in a cloud of dust, and Menendez thought he was a civilian until the men of Dog Company, with their rifles and machine guns, brought his vehicle to a halt.

A civilian would have been at least a little bit frightened to see the high intermountain grassland suddenly produce a crop of full-armed men. The newcomer wasn't scared by their appearance at all—if anything, he seemed pleased.

"Major Will Boone, Army Special Operations," he said, in response to Menendez's demand for his identity. "And you must be the officer in charge of Dog Company."

Menendez let that go unanswered. "Let's see your ID, Major Boone."

The man shook his head. "I'm traveling without. Is Hector Brazelton still with you? He'll vouch for me."

"Maybe," said Menendez. He turned to a man with LUCCA embroidered above his pocket and a sergeant's chevrons and rocker pinned to his collar. Sergeant Lucca was cradling a Squad Automatic Weapon and watching Boone, the road, and the lieutenant all at once. "Have somebody go get Heck."

The sergeant nodded to a younger man, who backed away, then faded into the brush. Some minutes passed in uncomfortable silence before the soldier returned, accompanied now by a large black man, dressed in cammies with a medic's red-and-white armband.

"Lieutenant?" the medic said.

"Yo, Heck," Menendez said, "this guy here says you know him. What's the scoop?"

"He looks like a guy named Boone that I used to know," Brazelton said. "But that doesn't prove anything anymore." He frowned in thought for a moment, then spoke to Boone. "We used to play poker together, back during the Israeli-Iraqi War, you and me and another guy. Who was the guy, and what finally broke up the game?"

"Iraq . . . the Megiddo Campaign. That would have

been Eddie," the newcomer said. He laughed. "And we had to stop playing when your pet goat ate all the cards except the joker and the three of clubs."

Brazelton glanced over at Lieutenant Menendez. "It's him all right, sir."

Menendez nodded, and turned to address the newcomer again directly. "Welcome to Dog Company, Major Boone. You're lucky that you made it up the road. It's mined all to hell."

—text of message sent from Kate Boone to Major William Boone via the United Nations Expeditionary Force Network (UNEF.Net)

Dear Will —

This has been a horrible week. Well, not in comparison with the kind of week you've doubtless been having lately, but you know what I mean. On a scale of grim to outstanding, this week would have to stand on a footstool to reach all the way up to mediocre.

For one thing, I have a cold. Not a little sniffly cold, either, but a honking, sneezing, coughing-and-wheezing full-blown monster of a cold. Everybody in the office has it. And I was the very first person to catch it, which also made me the first person to be back at work and sort-of functioning. [DELETED BY UNEF.NET SECURITY BOT] blames the office outbreak on [DELETED BY UNEF.NET SECURITY BOT] agents, but he blames everything on them, including global warming and the rise in public transit fares, so nobody takes him seriously.

Also the car broke down. I'd been trying to keep it going until I could get it looked at over the weekend, but this morning the engine choked, died, and refused to start. So it was public transit for me . . . I showed up at work half an hour late and found out that there was nobody holding the fort at the office except me and the Octopus and [DELETED BY UNEF.NET SECURITY BOT]. Everybody else was still at home sneezing.

So I spent all morning and most of the afternoon hunched over my workstation like a gargoyle on a waterspout, waiting for the day to be over so I could go back home and curl up with a box of tissues and a good book. (I'd much rather curl up with =you,= of course, but I'll take what I can get.) Nothing was happening, after all, just the usual bushel baskets full of data coming in for processing. Dump the numbers into the hopper, sort them a couple of times, and send them on to the next station. The kind of day where a trained monkey could have handled everything and still had time for a banana break. And it went on for hours.

Finally the Octopus started putting on his hat and coat. [DELETED BY UNEF.NET SECURITY BOT] and I perked up and looked hopeful, because he's too nice a guy to cut out early and leave the rest of us behind to suffer.

And wouldn't you know it, right about then my workstation went crazy. All the alarms I'd set up—the [DELETED BY UNEF.NET SECURITY BOT] and the [DELETED BY UNEF.NET SECURITY BOT] and the cross-check for [DELETED BY UNEF.NET SECURITY BOT]—went off at once, beeping and flashing and whistling.

"Um," I said to the Octopus. "I think you'd better look this over."

He came over to my workstation and took a look. He didn't think it was going to be anything important, I could tell, because he didn't bother to take off his coat. Five hours later, he still hadn't taken it off, and the three of us were rechecking every bit of incoming data we'd processed since the start of the project. This time we had the filters for [DELETED BY UNEF.NET SECURITY BOT] and [DELETED BY UNEF.NET SECURITY BOT] set a whole lot higher . . . and yes, we definitely had something.

I still don't know what it is we've got, though. The Octopus never said. It's almost three-fifteen in the morning and I've only now gotten home. The Octopus was still at the office when I left. I think he's planning to sleep there.

Exhaustedly (but eternally) yours,
Kate

THREE

Some time later, Boone found himself sitting by the campfire with the officer and NCOs of Dog Company, eating chunks of spit-roasted mutton and drinking the execrable local tea. The tea came from a hard black brick wrapped in red and gold paper; it had most likely been a legitimate purchase, made at some point before Dog Company vanished from sight. About the provenance of the mutton, Boone judged it best not to inquire too deeply.

"Looks like you guys are doing pretty well for yourselves," he said, wiping grease from his chin. "Any problems that I need to know about?"

"Just jump in that pile-of-dirt truck and haul out of here," Menendez said. "When we need help we'll call for it."

Boone was silent. The silence dragged on. After a while, Sergeant Lucca spoke up. "Dammit, sir, we didn't want to get found. How did you find us?"

"You went dark," Boone said. "Some people got worried. So I went to your last known location, and started scouting from there. Easy as that."

"Couldn't have been *that* easy," another sergeant—TOFFLER, according to his name tag—said in an aggrieved tone. "We tried to cover our tracks."

"That's what I was looking for," Boone said. "The way tracks are covered, if you know that there should have been tracks to start with, can tell you a whole lot."

Another silence, while the fire crackled. Menendez looked at his watch. "Satellite pass plus thirty."

"Yes sir," Lucca said, and upended a bucket of water onto the fire. He stirred the ashes to make sure they were out. "I'll inspect the site."

"Very well."

Lucca vanished into the dark. Menendez stood and nodded toward Boone.

"Let's talk. Want to take a walk?"

"Sure," Boone said. He pushed himself upright and finished his last mouthful of tea, then let Lieutenant Menendez lead him a few paces away from the camouflaged encampment. Even this short distance away, it was all but invisible in the dark. With the fire doused, not even the distant and godlike eyes of the orbital spy satellites would catch it.

"Major," Lieutenant Menendez began as soon as they were out of earshot of the rest of the company. His voice was low. "You aren't anywhere in my chain of command. My troopers are very loyal. Once we get out of here, they'll tell any story that I want 'em to tell—assuming that anyone even asks. And it would be a real tragedy if you were found dead next to a burned-out, blown-up vehicle. That road really is mined. The next guy won't find us as easily. So tell me: What were your complete orders?"

"To find Dog Company," Boone said. "To bring back either your ID tags or your report. That's it."

"They didn't tell you anything else?"

"No. What else is there?"

Menendez didn't answer for a long time. "We found a twonky."

Twonky. SpecOps slang for an object spectacularly out of place with regard to either time or location. Finding one was almost always a harbinger of trouble. "You reported that?"

"Yeah. Then the rest came up, and we decided that transmission was too risky. When I make my report, it'll be in person."

"Tell me about the rest."

"First let me show you the twonky."

Boone shrugged. "Okay."

"In the morning. We have some hiking to do. You don't think I'd put my camp near something like that?"

"No, Lieutenant," Boone said. "They told me you're good at what you do. We'll look in the morning."

"Right. I'll show you your doss. Don't move while one of the spy birds is over the horizon. No fires, no lights. You know the drill."

"Ay-firm."

Boone and Menendez walked back toward camp through the rocks and low thorn bushes. The place where Boone was set to sleep was between two boulders, with a natural overhang, and cammo netting slung above—not a soft bed, but as safe a one as he'd find in hostile country, with satellites sweeping by overhead. He settled in to sleep. But before he did, he pulled out his global from an inner pocket of his jacket, slid it open, and called the blind drop.

"Rover, bingo," he said. Then he slid shut the communicator and rolled up in his blanket.

During the night he thought he heard something metallic hit a rock nearby, and it brought him straight awake but unmoving. Sentry, he thought. The noise wasn't repeated, and by and by he went to sleep again.

* * *

Morning was only a gray promise on the horizon when Lucca came by and tapped on a canteen cup with a pencil to wake Boone and get his attention.

"Lieutenant's compliments, and time to saddle up, Major. You guys have some klicks to cover."

Boone rolled to his feet and pulled on his jacket. "Give me five minutes and I'll be in step."

The sergeant dumped a bundle of clothing at Boone's feet. "Cold-weather gear," he said by way of explanation. "You'll need it up where you're going."

The garments—a hooded snowsuit, insulated gloves, snow goggles—were somewhat too large for Boone, and he suspected that they'd previously belonged to Hector Brazelton. He pulled them on over his regular clothing anyway. Right now they were too warm, even in the predawn chill of the high intermountain meadows; once up in the snowfields, though, he would need that warmth.

He'd just finished dressing when another shape, lighter gray against the darker background, appeared in the morning light and spoke to Sergeant Lucca. Menendez's voice said, "Thanks, Sarge. Get a patrol ready to come with us. One day's rations. Break camp here, resettle at the next spot."

"You're not taking any chances," Boone commented.

"No sir," said Menendez. "Would you?"

"No. Lead the way, Lieutenant."

As Sergeant Lucca had promised, the hike was a long one. Boone followed Menendez and a dozen men from Dog Company up progressively steeper and more rocky hillsides, making their way out of the high meadows and onto the lower slopes of the snow-capped mountains. The early morning sunlight poured into the valley below them like honey, and glinted off the white crags above.

By noon they were well above the grass line and into a world of unmelting snow, carved by wind and sunlight into strange hummocks like kneeling figures or cathedral spires. The drifts were glittering white in the sun and azure-purple in the shadows, and the sky overhead was a clear and pitiless blue. A brisk wind coming off the high slopes made Boone grateful for his borrowed winter gear.

Shortly after midday, they came to a place where bare rock thrust its way through the snow and ice. A darkness amid the boulders marked what Boone took to be a cave entrance.

"In there, sir," Menendez said. "We picked it

up doing radio frequency direction finding. We'd been switching around the AM and FM bands without hitting a lot that we didn't already have mapped and broken, when Franklin decided to try and jury up a phase modulation receiver because he was bored. Darned if there wasn't a line. So we took a bearing, moved, got a cross, and got a fix up here.

"Weirdest damn thing I'd ever seen. Not high power. Why don't you take a look and tell me what you think?"

Boone nodded and ducked his head as he entered the cave. The cave was shallow, formed from tumbled boulders and slabs of rock, and high enough for a man a little shorter than Boone to stand in at full height. Against the far wall, where natural light could still hit it, stood a box, perhaps three feet on a side, made of overlapping gold and silver plates. It wasn't a true cube, but more of a truncated pyramid, flat on top and bottom with four sloping sides, each of a different angle.

Boone pulled out his pocket camera and took shots of the box from the front, two of its four sides, and the top. He didn't touch the box himself.

When he emerged from the cave, blinking against the stronger light, he said to Menendez, "I suppose you analyzed the signal?"

"Yeah, much as we could. There's some kind of nonrandom patterns, but nothing we could break in the field. Want to know the weird part?"

"I'm all ears," Boone said, as the patrol made its

way back down the slope. The patrol was returning to camp via a different path than they had taken in order to go up and view the twonky. Boone estimated that they would be coming out about five kilometers from where they'd started, over to the southeast of the original location.

"After we found that piece of gear, we started poking around a little more in the PM bands, and bet you'll never guess what we found."

"You're right, I'll never guess."

"Carrier signals," Menendez said.

"No kidding."

"Would I lie to you, Major?"

"Everybody lies to SpecOps," Boone said. "So what did you do next?"

"We did some DF. And get this, sir—one of the stations was off-earth."

"Satellite?"

Menendez shook his head. "Not that we could tell. Franklin said his best guess would put it somewhere on the back side of the moon."

"That's . . . interesting," said Boone. If any of the players in the current conflict had a working moon station at all, he hadn't heard so much as a whisper to that effect. "Go on."

"Franklin also said that the signal source had to be moving faster than light. A signal from moon space, followed by a signal from Mars space, less than eight minutes apart."

"That's not possible."

"Yeah," said Menendez. "I know."

"You're sure it's not coming from two different stations?" Boone asked.

As far as he knew, nobody on Earth had a Mars base, any more than they had a lunar one. But if he hadn't heard about a farside moon station, then he wouldn't have heard about a Mars base either—and he wasn't yet willing to discount the possibility of unmanned signal beacons in either spot.

"Franklin says it's just one. And where they seem to be sending stuff, and getting material back from, is trans-Plutonian space."

"Pluto," said Boone. Great. I don't care what they aren't telling us mushrooms, *nobody* has anything running out that far. "You're sure about that?"

"Who can be sure of anything?" Menendez said. "But the sequence—which we can't break, by the way—follows with an interruption. No way to synchronize—"

He broke off when the man on point, up ahead, held up his hand, then squeezed it into a fist: the signal for *halt*. The whole patrol, Boone included, froze in their tracks. Sergeant Lucca pointed to two men, then pointed to his own eyes, then to a spot up to the right, overlooking the trail ahead: *You and you. Go look over there.* The two soldiers crawled away, their cammo uniforms blending into the shadows before they'd gone more than a few yards.

Meanwhile, the point man dropped back to join the two officers and the senior NCO.

"What you got, Henry?" Lucca asked, low-voiced.

"Smelled something. Fuze wire."

"Okay."

They waited, hunkered down. The two scouts returned. "Looks clear ahead," one of them whispered.

"Okay, fire teams in diamonds, on an echelon left," Menendez said. "Heads up, everyone. Assume we're moving to contact."

The soldiers of Dog Company began moving out in groups of four, barely in sight of one another, along a diagonal stretching out downslope to Boone's right. It wasn't long before the four men in the lead team went to ground, concealing themselves behind rocks and bushes and in depressions in the earth. The rest of Dog Company came up slowly, weapons at the ready.

"What thing?" Menendez asked.

"There was an ambush here, couple of hours ago," Lucca said, scanning the ground. "Got some brass here, Chicom stuff. Over here, some NATO seven point six two. That's where some command-detonated claymore mines were set—probably what Henry smelled. Blood pools, two big ones, one little one. The guys who got caught took some hits. No casualties remaining on scene. So either the ambushers took prisoners, or the ambushees retired in good order."

"This spot is on the direct path from our last camp to our new one," Menendez said.

"Don't I know it," said Lucca. "Looks like our guys got hit."

Menendez glanced over at Boone. "A stranger shows up, and the next day we run into an ambush. Not good."

A number of the other men were also looking hard at Boone—and not with friendly expressions, either. After a moment the one whom Lucca had earlier addressed as Henry said, "Last night, sir, the Major here called out."

There was a moment of tense silence.

"We are dark," Menendez said to Boone. "Total EMCON. This is why. Hand it over."

Boone withdrew his global from his jacket pocket—moving with exaggerated slowness, so as not to make any inadvertently threatening moves in the presence of so many heavily armed men with itchy trigger fingers—and held the small device out to the lieutenant. Menendez took it, examined it dubiously, and looked back at Boone.

"Do I need to have you searched? Sir."

"No," Will said. "That's all there is to it."

"Who did you talk to?"

"My chain of command. Transmission time under five seconds. I reported the fact of contact."

"I hope that was it," Menendez said. "Right now, the only things saving your life are that Heck vouched for you and I'm feeling softhearted."

The lieutenant placed Boone's global against the base of a tree, stepped back five yards, and drew his sidearm, a nine millimeter semiautomatic. He took aim and fired, emptying the magazine into the rectangle of metal and plastic at the foot of the tree. The echoes rolled among the hills.

"The next guy who comes along following your trail can read that sign," Menendez said. He dropped the empty magazine and replaced it with a full one from his belt pouch. "Okay, everyone, move out. Let's see who's waiting at the rendezvous spot."

To Boone he said, "Don't think you're magic, SpecOps man. This is the field. Lots of things happen here."

The patrol formed up in open order and moved away downslope. Boone noted that Menendez was walking behind him now, and hadn't reholstered his pistol.

—text of message sent from Kate Boone to Major William Boone via the United Nations Expeditionary Force Network (UNEF.Net)

Will, oh Will —

Things have gotten very strange.

We have an armed guard outside the door at work now, and he—mostly he; a couple of times this week it's been a she—searches all our bags on the way in and on the way out. Looking for [DELETED BY UNEF.NET SECURITY BOT], maybe, but I don't think so. Nobody's going to do anything bad to [DELETED BY UNEF.NET SECURITY BOT], he's not important enough. I'm not important enough, either. And the Octopus is too nice a guy to have that kind of enemies.

They're not worried about =us=, I think is the answer. They're worried about that big pile of sorted and resorted data. Nobody takes the data out of the office—no printouts, no removable media, no nothing—and nobody brings anything in that might hurt it. Which was the rule all along, of course. But now they're really tough and fanatical about enforcing it.

And we keep on getting visitors. That never happened before, either. But we weren't important then, and now for some reason we are. The Octopus brings all these strange people in past the guard—they get searched and ID-checked both ways, the same as us peasants—and shows them what we've pulled together so far out of that big mass of numbers, and then he and his visitors vanish into his private office for hours and hours and come out looking . . . I don't know what the right word is. Scared is definitely a big part of it. But the other part . . . it's like a kid who's beginning to believe that there really is going to be a pony under the tree on Christmas morning.

And you know something, Will? =That= scares the hell out of =me=.

Love and shivers
Kate

FOUR

The sun was setting by the time Boone and the patrol from Dog Company came down off the rocky slope into the rolling grassland. Long shadows of the mountains filled the valleys, and the light was like golden amber. The soldiers in the patrol walked in silence, each one keeping barely within visual range of the others. No one had spoken for some hours—not since the lieutenant had said, "Rally point alpha," and the sergeant had taken a bearing with his compass and gestured for the patrol to move out.

Boone walked in the center of the formation, like a man under guard. He made no effort to do otherwise. He was pretty sure that if he tried to break away from the main group, he'd be shot before he made a dozen paces. And at the moment, he was the only soldier present who wasn't armed.

Things could change in a hurry, though; and with night falling, unless the rally point was close, they'd have to bivouac shortly. Looking around, he tried to form a mental map of their location.

Up ahead, scarcely visible in the brush that now

covered the hillsides, Sergeant Lucca held his hand up in a fist. Boone halted, and looked back at Lieutenant Menendez's position. The lieutenant had vanished. A moment later, Boone felt a touch on his shoulder. It was the lieutenant.

"Come forward with me," Menendez said, in a tone so low it wouldn't have carried more than a few feet. Then he dropped and commenced to belly-crawl downslope toward the sergeant's position. Seeing no point in protest—and much wisdom in doing as he was told—Boone followed suit.

Meanwhile, the quality of the light was changing. They'd have full dark in a few minutes. Boone kept the lieutenant in sight as he snaked his way forward between rocks and scrub to the sergeant's position.

"Go to the road," Sergeant Lucca said, as soon as the two officers were squatting beside him. "Landmark one. Good a place as any to hunker down."

"Roger that," Menendez said. "Set a perimeter."

Lucca stepped away and vanished, his cammo clothing and silent movement combining to make him undetectable. Boone and Menendez took shelter near a jumble of rocks and ate a cold supper of dry MREs washed down with water from their canteens.

The night passed interminably. Every once in a while a satellite in polar orbit traced its way across the sky, a bright moving dot against the distant stars. Boone huddled with his back against a rock for warmth, without noticeable success, and slept fitfully. Every time he opened his eyes, he saw Lieutenant Menendez sitting against an opposite rock, watching him. When grey light filled the sky, outlining the mountains to the east even while the western peaks remained in shadow, Menendez stood, stretched, and spoke again: "Move out."

They crossed the road, a dusty single-track that wove along the flattest way between two valleys. The last man across rubbed out the traces of their crossing. From there, the patrol found a stream, followed it until a peculiar formation of hills opened to the south, then made for the saddle between two equally spaced knobs. Again, Boone noted distances and landmarks as best he could along the way.

At last they came to a field amid the mountains, where lichens covered the gray rock and grass grew among the thorns. A streamer of water trickled down across the rocks from a spring a little way above.

"Rally point," Lucca announced. "Sweep it."

The patrol members spread out and walked the area. One by one they returned and reported to the sergeant, their message always the same: "Negative sign."

Boone stayed beside Lieutenant Menendez. He refilled his canteen from the spring, and stayed silent.

At last the sergeant reported to Menendez, "Negative sign, sir," and Menendez replied, "Tactical positions."

Boone followed the lieutenant up to a position overlooking the field, near the water supply. Once again, the men settled in to wait. The afternoon wore on.

After a while Boone asked, "All your men know how to find this place?"

After a few moments, Menendez said, "Yes."

"And all of your men know about the twonky?"

Again the pause, and then Menendez said, "Yes."

"Got the results of your investigations written down?"

"Negative," said Menendez. "Different men have different parts memorized."

The lieutenant didn't sound like he planned to be more forthcoming; quite the opposite, in fact. Boone lapsed back into silence. Later, as the sun was going down, Boone spoke again. "How long do you plan to wait here?"

"Awhile."

Darkness fell, and the stars came out. Toward the middle of the night, Boone woke to a faint but insistent popping noise—the sound of distant small-arms fire, not loud, but sufficient to bring him out of sleep. He tapped Lieutenant Menendez with his foot to wake him.

"Listen."

The lieutenant held his breath, then nodded, his face pale in the starlight. "Some NATO weapons. Good fire discipline. Some Sinos." He paused. "Also good fire discipline."

"Know of any friendlies in the area?"

Menendez shook his head. "Negat."

"Then that's your guys. They're in trouble; this group can make a difference."

"A rendezvous at night in the middle of a hot fire-fight? Are you nuts?"

"Some people say yes," Boone said. He got to his

feet and pulled on his gear. "Get your men; move out."

"You *are* nuts," Menendez said, standing also and moving to face Boone down as he spoke. "We're sitting tight."

"Lieutenant, you're in the Army, same as me. My oak leaf beats your bar. Now get going."

"You're a prisoner, sir. Until I say different you're a spy."

"Oh, hell," Boone sighed. "I'd hoped it wouldn't come to this." He snapped out his right hand.

When Lieutenant Menendez woke up, with an ache in his head, a taste of blood in his mouth, and his spirits full of a sense of impending doom, Major Boone was gone. Also gone, the lieutenant found when he checked, were a rifle, two loaded magazines, a map, and a compass.

Thinking about it, Menendez found that he wasn't terribly surprised.

* * *

At that same moment, Boone was two miles to the northeast, moving quickly and silently. He carried the stolen rifle—a NATO standard 7.62mm—at port arms as he ran through the night. A man with his eyes adapted to the dark can see well enough by starlight, provided he remembers to use only his peripheral vision.

Boone was guiding on the noise of weapons-fire. Sound is elusive, especially in the hills. Echoes can change direction, making the distant seem near and the near seem distant. But as soon as he was able to make out the glow of tracer rounds coming from beyond a low range of hills up ahead, he knew he was on the right track.

He hadn't been completely forthcoming earlier, when the lieutenant had asked him about his orders. It wasn't Dog Company he had to extract, it was their data—and Lieutenant Menendez, either on purpose or by coincidence, had made certain that the latter could not be retrieved without also rescuing the former.

Mini-discs would have been easier, Boone grumbled to himself as he ran toward the sounds of the fight. Or index cards. Or notes scrawled on the insides of chewing-gum wrappers . . . .

From up ahead came the *crump* of mortar rounds, incoming. Sixty mike-mikes. Boone switched off the safety on his weapon.

* * *

Master Sergeant Birki, acting company commander of Dog Company in the absence of First Lieutenant Menendez, had problems of his own. He had two men down, hurt bad in this morning's ambush; the lieutenant was still somewhere out of comms; and now Birki and the rest of Dog Company were encircled by hostiles.

The scouts Birki had sent out earlier reported that Dog Company was completely surrounded. The soldiers of Dog Company were shooting back, but keeping the rate of fire low. They were at the end of a long supply line; every round fired was one that couldn't be replaced until after they'd remade contact with the outside world.

After shooting their way out of the earlier ambush, Dog Company had made for the planned next night's bivouac by a circuitous route, hoping to find the lieutenant and his patrol already there. After waiting a decent interval for the lost squad to rejoin them, Birki decided to make a reconnaissance in force to the rally point, in case the lieutenant had run into trouble and needed to run. He put the two severely wounded soldiers into a cave overlooking the campsite, with a sniper to watch after them, and headed out.

That had been some hours before. Now Dog Company was taking fire from all points of the compass; only sporadic harassment and interdiction, now that it was dark, but still enough to keep everyone's head down.

They're trying to keep us pinned, Birki thought. *Maybe they're trying to take us alive.*

An uncomfortable thought, given the information that Birki and some of his men held in their memories, but one that had to be entertained. There was no telling if this was the good guys or the bad guys out there. In the midst of a shooting war—and the Sino-Indian Conflict was the biggest and nastiest shooting war to come down the pike in some decades—UN peacekeepers were unpopular with both sides.

Master Sergeant Birki could think of a number of reasons why people might want to shoot at Dog Company. Possibly the local inhabitants didn't want UN forces tramping heavy-footed all over land they thought was theirs. Possibly they wanted Dog's ammo and supplies, to augment their own meager stores. Worst-case, they wanted hostages, or the information the hostages carried. The strange gold-and-silver artifact in its snowbound hiding place weighed heavily on Birki's spirit.

To add to his joy, someone off to the northwest started lobbing in mortar rounds. That was something on beyond harassment and interdiction. The thud and *crump* when the shells hit told Birki that these were high explosive rounds coming in, rather than gas or biological, which wasn't as much of a comfort as he needed.

"Spread out," he said to the nearest member of Dog Company; he could hear his order being passed in whispers through the rest of the group. "Spread out, or the same round will get everyone."

The mortar rounds started walking across the valley, each one hitting closer than the last as the mortar team adjusted their elevation a notch at a time. Birki tried to guess where the next round would hit.

It never fell. "Bastards are trying to play with our minds," he muttered.

Then the northwest sky lit up with a flash like heat lightning, except too low and too close. An instant later a wave of sound rolled over the hiding troopers.

Looks like they dropped one in their own ammo, Birki thought. But if the troopers of Dog Company believed that they'd escaped, the ring of encircling troops disabused them of that notion by starting up a hot fire from all points.

"Down!" Birki shouted.

He fired two quick off-hand shots at a cluster of muzzle flashes about fifty meters to the east, and low-crawled to another location nearby. The thorns tore at him, but the rocks were his protection. A round struck one and went ricocheting off with a high, whining sound.

Birki fetched up against a boulder that would have been waist-high if he'd been standing. He leaned back against the rock, putting its bulk between himself and enemy fire, and glanced at his watch. The luminous numbers told him that only four hours of night remained. And dawn would bring no relief.

He considered his options. Dog Company could fight on, surrounded, until they ran out of ammo. Then they'd surrender and turn up in a mass grave somewhere, to the horror of the international press when it was discovered some months later. That wasn't a good choice.

Or they could break out and run like rabbits in the hope of making it back to civilization, or at least to territory occupied by non-openly-hostile civilians. That way, at least a few members of the company might survive.

A breakout at first light it would be, then. One direction was as good as any other. Birki chose east.

"Zero-five-thirty," Birki whispered to the man beside him sharing the cover of the boulder, "we're breaking out to the east. If you get separated, make your way individually to the rally point. Pass it on."

To his surprise, the man whispered back, "I've got a path cleared for you if you want to get out now."

It was the tall SpecOps major who'd showed up two days before. He was wearing borrowed cammies—Hector Brazelton's, it looked like—and carrying a rifle he must have picked up from one of the dead.

Birki stared at him. "Say what?"

"Gather your troops, Sergeant. Move from this point on a bearing one-zero-five for a thousand meters, then turn to due east for another thousand. From there, go to your rally point. Lieutenant Menendez is waiting for you there. Try to make it before dawn."

"Sir!" Birki said. "As soon as they notice we're gone, there's going to be unfriendlies looking all over the place."

A burst of fire came from outside the camp, answered by a sprinkling of shots from within.

"They won't notice," Boone said.

He placed the rifle he'd been carrying on top of the boulder, then unslung first one submachine gun from his shoulder, and then a second, laying them beside the rifle.

Those were never ours, Birki thought. He must have taken them from the enemy.

Next to the submachine guns the SpecOps major laid out four grenades, dark patches in the starlight.

"I'll pretend to be the lot of you," he said. "You have your orders, Master Sergeant. Gather your guys and move out. You've got some ground to cover."

"Yes sir," Birki said.

Dog Company headed out. For two full kilometers, Birki could hear the gunfire behind him. The major was indeed doing a good imitation of a full company.

The sky was shading up from deep gray to blue by the time Master Sergeant Birki and the main body of Dog Company rejoined Lieutenant Menendez's patrol at the hidden rally point. To Birki's surprise, Major Boone was there as well, playing poker with the lieutenant and Hector Brazelton.

"What took you?" he said. He folded the cards in his hand and raised his voice to carry to the whole company.

"Listen up, everyone. I'm taking command, and I'm extracting this unit. First we're going to retrieve our wounded. Then we'll head for India, to the U.S. Consulate in Goa. Five minutes to clear camp—we've got some klicks to cover."

—text of message sent from Kate Boone to Major William Boone via the United Nations Expeditionary Force Network (UNEF.Net)

Dear Will —

Now I know how Alice felt when she fell down the rabbithole. Just when I start to believe that life can't get any stranger, something happens to change my mind.

I can get used to never knowing exactly what it is I'm supposed to be looking for. I can get used to working under armed guard. I can even get used to having Distinguished Scholars and Very Important People parading in and out of the office while I'm trying to do my job.

But today . . . today it was visitors again. They came by the office early, around [DELETED BY UNEF.NET SECURITY BOT], while I was still finishing the carry-out breakfast I'd grabbed on my way in to work.

I heard them talking outside in the hall, a good thing because it gave me time to brush most of the doughnut crumbs off of my desk and toss the orange juice carton into the garbage before the visitors came in. Which they eventually did, of course—and

[DELETED BY UNEF.NET SECURITY BOT] took one look at them and turned pale.

Not surprising, really. He's the one with the thing about enemy agents, after all, and you don't need [DELETED BY UNEF.NET SECURITY BOT]'s official biography to tell you that he's been a loyal citizen of [DELETED BY UNEF.NET SECURITY BOT] for practically forever.

It really =was= [DELETED BY UNEF.NET SECURITY BOT], though, along with a full complement of muscular gentlemen in civilian suits and government-agent shoes. (Where =do= they get those shoes, anyway? Is there a cobbler's shop in Langley, Virginia, that advertises bespoke footgear to the trade?) Some of the extras looked like they'd come over on the same plane with [DELETED BY UNEF.NET SECURITY BOT], and the rest of them looked like our guys in mufti.

Usually the Octopus makes a point of introducing me at some point during the Distinguished Visitor parade—"and this is Kate Boone, who first spotted the [DELETED BY UNEF.NET SECURITY BOT] anomaly"—but today nobody introduced anybody to anyone. The Octopus and the Distinguished Visitor went straight back to the O's private office and didn't emerge for ages and ages.

When they finally did come back out, [DELETED BY UNEF.NET SECURITY BOT] was wearing the same damned expression that all the others had worn, scared and delighted both at once.

He and the Octopus shook hands, very gravely, and the O said, "Good luck, Shark."

I hadn't known that the two of them were on net-handle terms, but it shouldn't have surprised me. It's pretty clear that whatever the Octopus does for a living now, he started out as some kind of hotshot scientist, and all of those guys know each other. Hell, they could have been teaching assistants together, thirty years or so back.

The Distinguished Visitor said, "And luck to you also."

"We'll both need it," said the Octopus. "We're almost out of time."

He still hasn't explained what he meant by that. But it doesn't matter, because I'm starting to figure it out by myself. And the more I think about it, the more I know that I only =thought= I was scared, before. Now—

—now I'm downright terrified.

Take care of yourself, Will—
Kate

FIVE

The journey out of the Hindu Kush took Dog Company almost two weeks.

The men of Dog Company were well trained, and had good morale. They moved quickly and quietly, always alert. They traveled at dawn and at dusk. During the day they hid from watchers on the ground and in the air, and at night they took shelter to avoid the surveillance satellites passing overhead. All the mountain passes would be watched and guarded. Boone avoided those as well, choosing instead to take Dog Company over terrain where only a very dedicated enemy would follow—and then only with very good reason.

Boone took the lack of air activity as a good sign. On the fourth day of their trek, as the evening shadows lengthened and the company prepared to head out again and move until the lack of light made travel dangerous, Lieutenant Menendez approached Boone privately.

"Sir," he said, "I've been thinking. About the other night. You were right."

With that, he walked away. Boone didn't allow himself to smile. He wanted to stay on Menendez's good side, after all; there was no point in alienating the man by seeming to gloat.

On the tenth day they began to descend into the inhabited regions of northeastern India. The UN troops were no more welcome on this side of the Sino-Indian conflict than they were on the other, but neither were the locals inclined to offer them armed resistance. Dog Company moved on, leaving as little trace of their passage as they could, until one evening they stood on a rocky hillside, overlooking the lights of a town.

Menendez gazed down at the warm lights. "What do you say we scout this one out, make contact with base?"

"I've heard worse ideas," Boone said. "Anyone here speak Hindi?"

"Everyone here's been through language school," Sergeant Lucca said. "Most of us twice, to pick up at least two of the local lingoes. So yeah, we have Hindi speakers."

"Okay," said Boone. "One Hindi and one Urdu speaker, then. Go in with some trade goods and see if you can liberate a global from somewhere. If you don't get back by dawn, we'll come find you."

"That'll sure be inconspicuous," Menendez said.

"It'll get some people's attention, and maybe get us relieved," Boone said. He wrapped a cammie scarf tighter around his neck. "None of the guys who have the info from the twonky go."

"I don't like it," Birki said. "We should all go in together. Enough of this sneaking around. We've got cash. I think we should go in, buy a global, buy a couple of trucks if we can, and get out of this forsaken hill country."

Boone considered the town thoughtfully. "You know, I *like* that. Lieutenant Menendez, any thoughts?"

"One way or another, it'll be over," the lieutenant said. "Let's go."

They formed up in open order, skirmishers and scouts first, then a vee formation, as they moved down the hill in the twilight.

On the edge of the town, they paused. The smells of smoke and cooking wafted past them, pungent with garlic and spices amid the odor of night-blooming flowers, reminding them that they'd been eating MREs for entirely too long. The two translators went forward and knocked on the door of a nearby house, a small stone building with a red-and-white-striped cloth awning over the front. Somewhere out of sight down the way, someone with a boom box was playing Finnish rock music, loud enough to carry.

The door opened a crack, and yellow light poured out. The two troopers talked animatedly with the man who stood at the door. They gestured, he gestured, and finally the door closed. The men walked back to the two officers.

"Well?" Menendez demanded.

"They talk Urdu in this burg," said the nearer of the two men—a private whose name strip read

RODGERS. "The guy says the war is over. 'It's all over.' That's all."

"Did you find out anything about trucks?"

"No, but there's a train, and a bus once a month. He isn't sure if either one is running now that the war's over."

"This is making less sense by the minute," Boone said. "How about a global? Does he know where we can get one? Does he even know what they are?"

"There's a telephone exchange a couple of miles down the road," the second trooper said. "That much he told us, but the guy said 'For what good it'll do you.'"

"Those were his exact words?" Boone asked.

The second trooper nodded. "To that effect."

"Then let's go in," Boone said. "But try to stay out of any ambush situations."

Lieutenant Menendez waved his hand forward. The troops moved from their places of cover and concealment, and walked on. This time they continued until well after full dark, following the road now instead of skulking along in the underbrush. Boone felt uncomfortable, and suddenly under observation—as if too many eyes were following him. The observers didn't feel unfriendly, but Boone knew well enough that they were not necessarily friends.

Dog Company covered the two miles to the telephone exchange in a little over an hour, taking care to maintain cover and watching out for mines, booby traps, and ambushes. Eventually they came to the building that the translators had indicated. It had a satellite dish on the roof, so some kind of comms were possible from it, anyway. The sign over the door had the universal sign of a handset and a bell, white on a blue background, beside the Urdu script.

"Okay," Boone said. "Teams of two. Secure the building, and let's see if we can wake up the embassy in Delhi."

The telephone exchange stood on one corner of a wide intersection. This was a nice neighborhood—all the walls were painted, or at least whitewashed, and the streets were paved. The other buildings nearby, a grocery and a bank among them, stood shuttered and dark. The telephone exchange had a power line going into it, but all the visible light seemed to be coming from fires: candles, lanterns, and hearths.

The door of the telephone exchange was shut and locked, the windows shuttered and barred. One of the men, a corporal named Ogilvie, went forward to the door and played with the locks. After some five or six minutes of manipulation he stepped back.

"Got it, sir."

The trooper to the right of the door pushed it open. The trooper to the left of the door went in, under cover of the weapons of the men outside.

"Clear," he shouted. The others walked in, leaving a perimeter guard behind.

"Light this place up," Boone ordered.

The wall switch didn't work. Working with red-lensed flashlights, they found the telephone switchboard, a row of booths with handsets, and a cashier's cage. Then a team exploring the back of the building reported, "Found a diesel generator."

"Check it for booby traps, then fire it up," Boone said. "I want power in here."

"Roger that, sir."

The sentry by the door sang out, "Civilians coming up the road! Group of five."

"Keep them out, use minimum force."

"You heard the guy," Menendez said. I don't want a war crimes trial, if it gets down to that."

"Looks like some kind of delegation," Boone said. "Guys in their Sunday best."

Boone watched from a concealed position inside the building as the group of civilians halted at a respectful distance. One of the men wore a long coat and a saffron-colored turban; he spoke in a loud, carrying voice. His words had authority in them, even though Boone couldn't understand what he was saying.

The corporal standing beside Boone and Menendez could understand him, though. "He says welcome to town, the war's over, please leave as soon as convenient."

"Great," said Boone. "Invite him inside. Just him alone. Search him for weapons and explosives before he goes through the door. Treat him professionally and respectfully, but don't take any BS off him."

"Yes sir."

With a cough and a roar, the diesel generator started up, and the lights in the ceiling—flyspecked fluorescent tubes—flickered to life. Four of the men, electronic communications specialists, faded back toward the switchboard and the transmission equipment.

The lead civilian was brought in by two of the junior men of Dog Company, briskly patted down, and taken inside. "This guy here is the local head man," the translator said to Boone. "I guess you'd call him the mayor."

"Good evening," Boone said, as the translator repeated his words in Urdu, if the villager had spoken Hindi, Boone could have spoken with him directly, "We are dreadfully sorry to trouble you and your town. We will cause no harm, and soon be on our way."

"Gentle sir," the civilian's words were translated. "I bid you welcome, and wish to assure you that the war is over. There is no longer need for weapons or violence."

"Got a carrier wave!" one of the techs shouted from over by the transmission gear.

"The war is over?" Boone asked the mayor, still speaking through the translator. It wasn't impossible—armed conflicts in the twenty-first century could spring up like dust devils on the Great Plains, and die down as quickly. Still, he'd figured this latest war for one of the other, long-lasting kind. "Who won?"

"No one, it is over, do you understand?"

"No, I don't. Tell me what happened."

"They said that soldiers might come who had not heard. God has arrived, and all is well."

"I don't recall hearing any trumpets," Master

Sergeant Birki said, but the translator didn't repeat his words.

"That's very good to hear," Boone told the mayor. "But still I need to contact my superiors. Then we will leave." He paused. "Tell me about God."

The mayor pulled from within his coat a picture—a postcard-sized painting, of a blue man sitting in a lotus position on a cloud. Rays of light proceeded from the man's fingers.

"The gods who arrived look like this," the mayor began.

"Got satellite lock-on!" a tech reported.

"Get me COMSPECWAR, D.C.!" Boone shouted back.

"And there will be no more war, nor hunger, nor disease," the mayor continued.

"No joy. No joy," said the tech. "Negative comms. No one seems to be talking."

Menendez was frowning over the tech's shoulder at the radio set. "The satellite's there, you've got a carrier, and you aren't getting anything?"

"Nothing. It's like the world's gone away."

"Sir," Boone said, interrupting the mayor's philosophical dissertation. "Does anyone in this town have a global?"

"A what?"

Boone took a piece of paper from his pocket and sketched the handheld communicator. "One of these."

"The doctor has such a thing, but . . ."

"Please, bring the doctor here, with his global. I have money, and can pay him for his time and trouble."

"With joy shall I do so," the man said. "But I fear it will do no good."

"Please," Boone said.

The mayor bowed, and was escorted from the building.

"Well, that was fun," Menendez commented. Four of the civilians, the mayor among them, waited outside, while the fifth departed. "If the next thing coming in is a mortar round through the roof, we can say 'oh, well.'"

"It's more than that," Boone said. "Albert Einstein said 'I don't know what weapons World War Three will be fought with, but World War Four will be fought with sticks and stones.' We may be between world wars."

"More likely some info virus hit the satellite, and it's under quarantine," Menendez said. "These guys are at the end of a long intel chain. With all the disinformation flying around, I'll bet they get the wildest of the wild stories."

"Do *you* believe that the world's ended and God is back?"

Menendez shook his head. "Nope."

"Then we act as if hostilities are still hot. We're the UN observer team. We do our job, we do it well, we get home."

"Roger that," Menendez said.

Now a pair of civilians was approaching the checkpoint outside—the man who had left earlier, and an older, shorter man, with a pointed beard and a droopy mustache.

"Bring them in and search them, Sergeant," Boone said to Lucca.

"Yes, sir."

The mayor, with the doctor beside him, approached the building, where the trooper searching them found only a global in the doctor's possession. After introductions had been made all around, Boone spoke to the doctor through a translator: "Please open your global, sir."

"With pleasure," the doctor replied, and did so.

"Now please punch in the following number—"

"Are you nuts?" Menendez whispered. "He might memorize it. There's our security right there."

"Relax," Boone told him. "It's my wife I'm calling—just to make sure the thing works, and doesn't blow up when someone tries to use it. If it's booby-trapped, it'll go in his hand, not mine."

By now the doctor had finished punching in the number. He held up the screen of the global where Boone could see it: nothing but a dark blue "SERVICE UNAVAILABLE, TRY AGAIN LATER," message, over the Doors International logo.

"As you see, Major," the doctor said. "So it has been, for all places."

Boone held out his hand, and took the global. Shielding the pad with his hand, he punched in the SpecOps drop code. A moment later, the same SERVICE UNAVAILABLE screen showed up.

"Okay," Boone said. He handed the global back to the doctor and turned to the mayor. "Your Honor," he said, "perhaps you can help me a little more. I need transportation to the nearest city with an American consulate for myself and my men. I am prepared to pay."

"Money is useless, now that God is here," the mayor said. "But I think that something can be arranged."

—text of message sent from Kate Boone to Major William Boone via the United Nations Expeditionary Force Network (UNEF.Net)

Will, my love—

Nothing is ever going to be the same again.

I wish I could explain what I just wrote, but I can't. Not yet. Even though by the time you actually read this, the whole world will probably know.

After the Shark came all the way from [DELETED BY UNEF.NET SECURITY BOT] so he and the Octopus could have a heart-to-heart talk, nobody at the office felt like pretending things were normal anymore. I sure didn't, anyhow. I was working myself up to approach the Octopus and ask him for some explanations—after all, I was the one who spotted the [DELETED BY UNEF.NET SECURITY BOT] anomaly in the first place—when he came over to my desk.

"Caitlin," he said. "Ms. Boone."

"Yes?" I must have sounded even more dubious than I felt.

"You've done excellent work for the Project—"

"Thanks," I told him.

If you want to know the truth, this was the first time I'd heard that what we had going was a Project.

All my paychecks ever said was "Department of [DELETED BY UNEF.NET SECURITY BOT]"—and they'd said =that= before the Octopus ever brought me to the [DELETED BY UNEF.NET SECURITY BOT] Building to work for him.

"Excellent work," he said again. "And some of us think it's about time you heard the whole story."

I thought so too, but that's not the kind of thing you can say to your boss, even if he =is= basically a decent guy. So I said, "Thanks," again—

— and then it was my turn to go into the Octopus's private office, and see the things and hear the things that our visitor from [DELETED BY UNEF.NET SECURITY BOT] had heard and seen. And now I know why he looked the way he did afterward, and now I know what he meant when he said there wasn't much time.

Is this how you feel, when you know things you can't tell me?

Whatever else changes, I'll always love you—
Kate

SIX

The bus from Norfolk, Virginia, was overdue.

Kate Boone waited in the main concourse of the Washington, D.C., bus depot, looking impatiently from her wristwatch to the wall clock to the arrival board over the door, then back again to her watch. The white-on-blue arrival board still listed the bus from Norfolk as ON TIME, in spite of direct evidence to the contrary.

The bus depot had been built during the Great Depression early in the previous century, and the building still possessed a kind of seedy grandeur. Like all the others of its kind, the depot had fallen upon hard times during the last few decades, but was currently undergoing a revival. Now that the space aliens had arrived, air travel was severely restricted. "A temporary measure only," all the government spokespeople said. Kate wasn't sure if the restriction was by the new arrivals' specific wish, or whether it was a matter of prudence on the part of the worlds' leaders. She didn't think it mattered, really. Either way, the effect was the same.

Whatever the cause, the old railway and bus and steamship lines were experiencing a resurgence. Americans in particular hadn't given up their love of travel, and there was no shortage of entrepreneurial types willing to cater to it.

Who knows, Kate thought. Maybe in a dozen years we'll be seeing rail barons again on Wall Street. Or maybe the planes will start back flying, and the boom will go bust. It's not really under our control anymore.

The sign flipped from ON TIME to ARRIVED.

Kate grasped her purse tighter. In spite of herself, she felt her muscles tense and her heartbeat accelerate. Will had been away for over a year this time, and the whole world had changed since she'd seen him last.

The joke among Army wives in the SpecOps community was "Ask your husband for a recent photo so you'll remember what he looks like." She remembered what Will looked like—but what if he'd changed when everything else did? And what about her? Was she still the same person he'd left behind?

The door from the bus ramp to the concourse opened, and people came through. Kate watched, being careful not to push forward. It wouldn't do to make a scene, not on one day's leave from the Project, even if her work there was winding down now that the aliens—the *Taelons*, she had to remember to call them by their proper name—now that the Taelons were officially present on Earth.

And then, there he was, a head taller than most of the people around him, a straight-backed man with square shoulders and a strong jaw, wearing the green Army Class-A uniform with major's stars on his shoulders. Above the breast pocket the left side of his chest was gaudy with service ribbons. He had a duffel bag clasped by its handle in one hand, and carried a briefcase in the other.

Just inside the door he paused to scan the concourse. Then he saw her. His face lit up with a smile, like a beacon coming on behind his eyes, and he pushed through the crowd toward her. Katie raised a hand to wave, then ran forward herself, and never mind her dignity.

They met below the clock, with his arms around her, hers around him, and the briefcase and duffel bag abandoned beside them on the floor. Her purse swung from its shoulder strap, unheeded, as they kissed, deeply. After what seemed to be five minutes they came up for air.

"Oh, Will," Kate said at last, holding him and looking up into his eyes. "Where have you been?"

"I'm sorry," he said. "I can't tell you."

With that they both laughed. It was a joke of long standing between them, ever since Will had joined the Special Operations world and left ordinary soldiering behind—even though Kate's clearance was at least as high as his own. They both had Top Secret access modified with a long string of letters whose meanings themselves were classified, and Kate had, in the past, done work as secret as his, though hers was done at a civilian computer in an office cubicle rather than in exotic—if uncomfortable—parts of the globe.

"So what are we still doing here?" Kate said. "My car's out in the lot."

Will picked up his duffel and briefcase again. He let her link her arm through his as they made their way through the concourse, past the kiosks selling ice cream and newspapers and cut-rate floral arrangements.

"Got any plans for the afternoon?" he asked.

"I was thinking about hanging out at the bus station picking up sailors," she said, "but I didn't see any sailors. So I'm free."

"Then let's go for a drive."

"Where to?"

"Wherever you're staying. I want to go home."

Something in his voice . . . Kate paused and turned toward him. "Is there something wrong, Will?"

"In the car, Katie."

He moved purposefully across the floor to the exit. She had to lengthen her stride to keep up with him. Then they were outside, and across the parking lot. Only after they were inside the vehicle and moving, with the air conditioner humming and a chill breeze blowing from the vents, did she speak again.

"Was it rough?"

"No more than usual," he said. Then, "I've been fired."

"Discharged?" She had to fight down a surge of indignation on Will's behalf. "Well, *that's* the thanks of a grateful nation for you."

He shrugged. "I served at the pleasure of the president, and right now the president is pleased to have a lot fewer soldiers. So they gave me a Silver Star, a civilian readjustment allowance check, and orders allowing me to wear my uniform for twenty-four more hours or until I arrived home, whichever came first."

"What are you going to do?"

"Nothing much for right now," he said. "The civilian readjustment allowance is equal to about a year's pay. You'll still be working, so it's okay. I'll find something to do before long."

She frowned as she steered the car through traffic. The streets in downtown D.C. were as crowded as ever—no one, seeing them, would think that an alien invasion had taken place. And had succeeded, so smoothly and tidily that nobody ever used the word "invasion" to describe it at all.

"It still isn't fair," she said, after a long pause.

"I've seen some strange things, Katie, between India and here," Will said. "I've seen the desert blooming under the shadow of the pyramids, and people told me it was the Taelons who did it. If wars are caused by scarcity and hunger, then maybe there won't be war anymore and there isn't any need for guys like me."

"*I* need you," she said. "For now let's start at the basics. Let me take you home, get you a drink, and show you the rose bushes. They're lovely."

"Okay."

Another silence fell. They were like intimate strangers, Kate reflected, but this at least was nothing new. She was used to homecomings, and so was Will. They had been through long separations before, based on the needs of the service; and there was always a readjustment period, a time for settling into new quarters and rediscovering familiar identities. But now Will would be the one displaced, needing to find some kind of temporary job. His world had been knocked out from under him, far more than hers had been.

"Did you get my letters?" she asked at last. "I wrote nearly every day."

"I got them all in one big slug, on the ship back home from Egypt," Will said. "One huge download, once the comms were back up. They helped."

"You never wrote—"

"I never did," he agreed. "I wish I could have."

"—but I didn't let that bother me, because I knew that if anything bad happened to you, another major and a chaplain would appear on my doorstep to bring me the bad news. So as long as they didn't show up, I didn't worry."

"I'll be home every night from now on. I hope the sailors aren't too disappointed."

"There'll be mourning in the fleet, but they'll just have to cope. Me, I'll be overjoyed."

She took one hand off the steering wheel long enough to kiss her fingertips and then plant the kiss on his cheek. He caught her hand and kissed it again.

"Where are you living now?" he asked. He didn't let the hand go.

"In a house in Gaithersburg. I'm renting."

"Sounds like you're doing all right for yourself. Good job?"

"Didn't you read?"

"Yeah. There were parts missing."

"I'll tell you about them later. Right now I'm interested in something else that's been missing from my life for quite a while."

"I'll help you look for it," he said. "It may take us all afternoon."

"That's my man," Kate said, laughing. "I've got lots of frozen food at home. I have the rest of the day off, and the Octopus said he'd understand if I didn't make it in tomorrow."

They continued in silence for a minute more. Traffic was light, heading out toward the suburbs.

Then: "These blue aliens," Will said. "What do they say about them?"

"They who?"

"At the office."

"All I know," Kate said, carefully, "is what everyone else knows. They come in peace. They call themselves Taelons. They want to be our Companions. With a capital C."

"And they bring gifts," Will said. "You've heard the one about Greeks bearing gifts?"

"I've heard it," she said. "But the word from on high is that we're to treat them with total cooperation."

"That's because 'on high' knows that there's nothing we can do to defend ourselves against things that can travel interstellar distances, using who-knows-what for power sources. They could sit up there and drop washing machines out of their spaceships and devastate any country on Earth that resisted, so why bother to resist?"

She felt a stirring of dismay. "Will—don't talk that way. They're here, and there's nothing we can do about it."

"I've been to a lot of places," he said, ignoring her interjection, "and in a lot of those places my mission was to win the locals' hearts and minds. And I did. But you know what? Not one of those times was I doing it for their purposes. I was doing it for mine. And right now I'm waiting for someone to come running down the street waving one of the Companions' books in his hand and yelling 'It's a cookbook!'"

He paused. "I've seen pictures of their towers. Where's the one in D.C.?"

"Out near Georgetown."

"Take me over there. I'd like to see it in real life."

"Okay. It isn't too far out of our way. No one can get near it, though, without the right passes and permits."

"Just somewhere where we can see it."

Kate took a left, then continued on until they came to the on-ramp for the Beltway. They went west, then curved south. Then there it was: rising like a living thing, an undersea polyp of purple and gold, looming up huge and impossible above the skyline. It glistened in the sun, as if it were wet.

Will looked out of the window, his eyes hooded. "Okay," he said finally. "It's just like the videos. Let's go home."

Kate pulled off the ring road at the next exit, went under the highway, and headed in the opposite direction. Traffic was picking up now, at the end of the workday for the Washington bureaucrats. Soon they were in the suburbs in Maryland, heading toward Rockville, and at last coming up to the house that Kate had rented. Will had never seen it before.

"Well," she said, pulling into the driveway. "This is it."

"Where are the flowerbeds you wrote me about?"

"Around in back. But that isn't the kind of bed I had in mind."

"Woman of my dreams," Will said, laughing. He pulled the duffel from the trunk and the briefcase from the back seat and followed her to the door. The security plate beeped as she disarmed it, and they were in.

Kate kicked off her shoes and left them on the floor in the entryway. "I have ice-cream and cake in the fridge," she said, continuing on into the house and shedding her suit coat as she went. "Champagne, too. Want some?"

"Afterward," Will said. He stripped off his uniform jacket and tossed it across the back of the couch. "Guess I'll just be wearing this on Veterans' Day from now on," he said.

He loosened his necktie and tossed it on top of the jacket, and kept on going toward the stairs. Then his global signaled. He had to walk back over to the couch to get it out of his uniform pocket.

Kate paused at the foot of the stairs to listen, taking care to stand out of line-of-sight for the device's video pickup. She shouldn't be visible anyhow at this range—though she would be able to catch an off-angle glimpse of the on-screen image—but the emerging etiquette of live-video communication said that she should take the precaution.

Will pulled out the global's screen. Kate's heart sank when she saw that the caller wore an army uniform: in the service, nothing good ever came of unexpected phone calls.

They can't send him away again, she thought. They've already decided to let him go. It has to be something else.

"Major Boone," said the starched corporal in the picture.

"Not anymore," Will said. "I'm Mr. Boone now."

"As of zero-six-hundred tomorrow morning," the corporal said. He glanced down at something on his desk. "According to this list. In the meantime, sir, your presence is requested in the C-ring of the Pentagon, Room C-121."

"When?"

"As soon as convenient."

"It'll be convenient in about four hours," Will said. Then he looked up at Kate, and saw what she had done with the rest of her suit. "Correction," he told the corporal in the global. "Five hours."

—text of message sent from Kate Boone to [DELETED BY ARCHIVE SECURITY] at the office of the Extrasolar Research Project

You were right, boss. I'm not going to be coming in to work tomorrow.

Meanwhile, Will's been summoned for a visit to the Five-Sided Rat Cage, which doesn't exactly fill me with great glee. No good can come of being invited to call on the high and the mighty with fewer than eighteen hours to go before he says good-bye to the lot of them for once and for all.

That's right, today's big surprise was that he was supposed to be discharged—Silver Star (yes, I'm bragging about it, because he never will) and severance pay and a hearty handshake, which is about the least they could do, considering. Nothing is too good for our boys in the service; it's just that Congress hasn't figured out how to give them less than nothing yet. All in all, I wasn't nearly as rattled by the news as he was, and I could definitely get used to him being at home for more than a month at a stretch. I mean, if I hadn't liked having him around the house I wouldn't have married him to start with.

But I know what's going to happen. In a couple of

hours somebody I've never met is going to say, "Major Boone, duty calls," and my husband's going to say, "Sir yes sir," and there he'll go.

Which is sort of the long way around to saying that I may not come in to work the day =after= tomorrow, either. If I've only got a little time with Will before he disappears again, I intend to make the most of it.

Thanks for understanding—
K. B.

SEVEN

Most of the military personnel who worked in the Pentagon wore mufti. Major Will Boone—who'd worked in civilian clothing more often than not during his time in the field—elected instead to wear his uniform for his final visit. He emerged from the Metro station and made his way via the underground passageway to the checkpoint in the basement of the A-ring. He presented his ID chip.

"Yes sir," said the Marine sergeant on duty, and consulted the data terminal in front of him. "You're expected, sir."

"Thank you," Boone said.

He made his way down the ramp to the corridor leading to the C-ring, halfway between the outside of the building and the inner ring where the highest ranking and most powerful officers had their offices.

Legend had it that the Pentagon had initially been planned during World War II as a military hospital, to accommodate the huge influx of wounded anticipated from the invasion of Japan. The building's extra-wide corridors were supposedly designed to handle hospital gurneys. Boone didn't know if the story was true.

In any case, the projected invasion had never taken place, due in part to the use of the atomic bomb. Boone thought it ironic that the United States, along with the rest of the world, had fallen this time to an invasion in which there had been no casualties and no weapons used.

Considering the nature of human beings, Boone reflected, maybe the new order of things was an improvement on the old. Or maybe it wasn't. He wished he could be certain which.

The Pentagon had been the biggest office building in the world for a long time. Even so, the place had been laid out so that any point in the building was within five minutes walk of any other. Very shortly, Boone came to a stairway and, rather than using an elevator, took the stairs to the first floor. Then he turned to his left and came to Room C-121.

Another marine stood outside the door. She looked at Boone's name tag, white letters on black plastic pinned to the right side of his chest, and said, "Sir." She swung the door open for him and stood aside.

Boone walked into the room.

The floor of Room C-121 was carpeted in green, and bookshelves lined the walls. No windows opened to the outside; the Pentagon was not a place for claustrophobes. A conference table with a series of computer monitors stood in the center of the room.

A man in a rumpled green suit sat at the table, reading papers in a looseleaf binder. The name tag dangling from his breast pocket bore the name JOHN SMITH in red letters next to the logo of the National Security Agency. He had a pencil in his hand, and made changes to the papers as he read.

An older officer, a colonel wearing the insignia of the signal corps, sat in a chair on the far side of the room. He looked up as Boone entered, but said nothing.

Boone took two paces into the room, stopped, saluted, and said, "Major Boone, reporting as ordered."

"Took you long enough," said the NSA man with the looseleaf binder. He didn't bother to glance up from his work. "Take a seat."

"Thank you," Boone replied, unruffled by the curt greeting, and pulled out a chair on the opposite side of the table. He'd encountered psychological ploys like that one before—had used them himself in the field, from time to time—and he didn't feel like giving Mr. Smith from the NSA whatever negative reactions he might have been probing for.

After a few moments, the NSA man stopped writing and looked up. His eyes were a frosty blue, and the expression on his face was equally frosty.

"Major Boone," he said. "Your activities over the last few months have been very interesting. Unfortunately, the information you brought back from your last assignment came too late to be of any help."

"I expect you've seen my report," was all Boone said.

"Yes."

A long pause followed, while Mr. Smith seemed to make up his mind. "Don't feel bad. It's unlikely that your information could have been of use even if it had been delivered instantly. You can still be useful to your country. Would you like to be?"

"I swore an oath to that effect," Boone said. "I haven't changed my mind."

"Very well. What is your opinion of the Taelons?"

"I was unaware that I was required to have an opinion. My understanding is that the president has ordered full cooperation with them."

"That is so. What is your private opinion?"

"That I'd like to see some benefit coming to them from their arrival. When anyone comes around talking about all the good things he's going to do for me, I wonder about his motives. Where's the hook in the worm?"

"Exactly so," Mr. Smith said. "Not everyone is convinced that the Taelons are kind and benevolent and lacking in ulterior motive. It would please me a great deal if you kept your mind open, as well as your eyes and your ears, and let us know anything that you think we'd like to know."

"And that would be?"

"Left to your best judgment."

"I suppose I could do that."

"Very well." Mr. Smith stood up. "I am not in your chain of command. Colonel Purcell, however, is. He will brief you."

Mr. Smith closed the looseleaf binder and left the room, leaving Boone and Colonel Purcell alone.

The colonel was the first to speak. "I've read your record, Major Boone—at least, the parts that weren't sealed for national security at a higher classification than I have myself. It speaks well for you."

No answer seemed to be called for, so Boone said nothing. Purcell went on. "You're currently scheduled for discharge . . . when?"

"As of zero-six-hundred hours tomorrow, sir."

"That's cavalier treatment for somebody who's done as much for his country as you have, wouldn't you say?"

Years of SpecOps training kept Boone's expression neutral, even though he knew a loaded question when he heard one. "Worse things have happened to better people," he replied. "I'm not a hardship case or anything like that—I have my civilian readjustment allowance to tide me over."

"Hm." Purcell looked at him for a moment. "Do you have a job lined up yet?"

"No, sir. But I've got time to look around."

"How do you feel about Denver?"

"Sir?"

"Colorado," Purcell said. "Mountains—close by, anyhow. Nice climate, if you don't mind the winters. The police force there has an opening for a lieutenant. It's yours if you want it."

"Police work," Boone said thoughtfully. Even though he still mistrusted the source, the offer was tempting. "I could handle police work."

Colonel Purcell nodded as if satisfied by his reply. "We thought you could. That's why we thought of you when we got word of the opening."

"You say 'we'", Boone commented. "Who's that, sir?"

"Think of us as a loose network of people who share your concerns about the Taelon arrival. Not strictly military, and not entirely civilian either."

"I'm not sure I'm up to joining anything new at the moment, sir."

"You wouldn't have to," Purcell said. "Except for the police force, naturally."

"This all sounds too good to be true," Boone said. *Kind of like the gifts of the Taelons, if it comes to that,* he thought, but he knew better than to make the comparison aloud. "So where's the catch?"

"No catch, Major. All we want is for you to do an honest job and keep your eyes open. People were knocked way off-base when the Taelons showed up—your record says you saw some of that for yourself—"

"In India. Yes, sir." Boone thought about the village doctor who had believed that Dog Company's money would do him no good, now that God had arrived. "People had some strange ideas."

"A lot of folks didn't know what to think," Colonel Purcell said, "and that was bad. Suicides, psychotic episodes, weird cults springing up all over—you would have been in transit during the worst of it. People have mostly settled down now. Unfortunately, they seem to have settled down into believing that the Taelons are Santa Claus, and from now on every day is going to be Christmas."

"I'm still not sure how this ties in with making me a lieutenant in the Denver police department."

"It gives us one more law enforcement officer who doesn't think that the sun only comes up in the morning because the Taelons get behind it and push," Colonel Purcell said. "There may come a day when we need all of those people we can get."

"'We' . . . are you talking about your 'loose network' again, sir?"

"No, Major. This time I'm talking about the human race."

"I understand," Boone said. And how many other soon-to-be-discharged soldiers, he wondered but didn't say, have you had this conversation with already? "What is it that I'd have to do?"

"Just show up for work and keep your eyes open," Purcell said. "And keep us in mind."

* * *

"So you have a job lined up," Kate Boone said a few hours later at the house in Gaithersburg, over their long-delayed celebration feast of ice cream and champagne.

"I told them that I'd have to check with you," Boone replied. He lifted another scoop of strawberry ice cream into his dish and drizzled chocolate sauce over it. "It would require moving."

"To where, to do what?"

"To Denver, to be a cop," Will said.

"You've never been a cop in your life. Isn't there a police academy or something? And why would you want to walk a beat? Why not be an investment banker and buy me a Porsche?"

"I'd start as a detective," Will said. "Not a beat cop. And the way it was explained to me, all I'd have to do is show up every morning. Sort of Uncle's way of saying 'Sorry we snatched that pension away from under your feet.'"

"I know you, Will," Kate said. "You've never been able to do a half-assed job in your life. If you take this one, you'll be going to the office early, working late, and hitting it with everything you have."

"I promise I'll do my best to slack off," Will said. He ate a spoonful of ice cream. "Are you in love with your work here in D.C.?"

"Not particularly," she admitted. "I'm not in love with this house, either. Where you go, there go I. You know that. But it's your life; don't make it be my decision. What did you tell them?"

"That I'd think about it."

"Until?"

"I have until zero-five-fifty-nine tomorrow to let them know."

Kate stirred the ice cream in her own bowl. "I'll tell the Octopus I'm leaving. The Project's finished, anyway. We found what we were looking for, and it's tall and blue."

"I'll be tall and blue too, in a cop suit," Will said.

Kate laughed, and put a dab of ice cream on his nose with her finger. "Call them now. You don't want to oversleep and miss the deadline."

"I won't oversleep."

"Yes, you will. If I have anything to do with it, you're not going to get out of bed for three days." She pushed his global across the table toward him. "If the job isn't what you want, you can quit and be a beachcomber, and I'll go comb the beaches with you. I know you, Will, and you want to do this, or you would have told them flat out no."

"You know me way too well," Boone said, and pulled out the global's screen to make the call.

—text of message sent by Kate Boone to [DELETED BY ARCHIVE SECURITY], Gaithersburg, Maryland, USA.

I have to say, it was quite a good-bye party. I didn't know you could get away with smuggling that much booze into a Washington office building. I swear even the Octopus got a little bit tiddly, somewhere about the time [NAME DELETED] and [NAME DELETED] were dancing on the tables.

My mother brought me up to be a good girl and always write my thank-you notes promptly, and I hear from my sources—from the Octopus, actually, as I was packing up my desk—that you were the mastermind behind the celebration. So consider yourself properly thanked, okay?

Will and I are going to take a nice leisurely drive across country to Colorado. I don't think we've had this much time together by ourselves in, oh, years and years. The Army kept him busy coming and going. Once we get to Denver, I'm not sure what I'll do. Take it easy for a while, most likely; I worked enough eighteen-hour days while the Project was in high gear to last me for several years at least. Maybe I'll do a bit of freelance work now and then to keep my skills from getting rusty.

I don't want to lose touch with the old gang completely, though. I can't say yet what my streetmail address and global code are going to be, but the net address stays the same—not the work address at the Project, of course, but this one. If you ever need to get in touch with me, it's the one to use.

Best of luck with everything—
Shrew

EIGHT

"Mackay, Mackay, what got ye to lie. 'Neath the bush on yonder bankie-o?"

Will Boone swung in his office chair and clicked off the radio. The folk music revival that had been clogging up the airwaves ever since the Taelon arrival wasn't making him any happier. The Denver cops were allowed to listen to civilian radio during working hours, on the off chance that some eyewitness listener would check in with word of a crime in progress, but so far this hour had been wall-to-wall banjos and bodhrans with never a newsbreak.

Boone refused to let the petty annoyance spoil his first day as the Denver police department's junior captain, or his enjoyment of the new office that accompanied the promotion. The office was pretty Spartan as yet—just the desk, the calendar, the phone, and the computer, plus one swivel chair behind the desk and one straight-legged chair in front of it—but it came with a glass-paned door that separated him from the noisy and overcrowded bullpen where he'd worked for the past two years as a police lieutenant.

He set down his clipboard full of unprocessed paperwork and pressed a button on his desk comp to retrieve and print the latest updates. Time to see what new malfeasance had arrived in the overnights.

The coming of the Taelons might have put a damper on global armed conflict, but it hadn't brought a slowdown in the world of police work. Sinful ginful rumsoaked men were still battering their wives, wallets were still being lifted, little old ladies were still being swindled out of their life's savings. It kept a man busy, tracing the perpetrators down and making them regret their misspent youths.

First up on the comp was the list of stolen vehicles from the night before. There'd been a plan in the works, back before the end of the last war, to install permanent markers on all vehicles so they could be tracked from orbit as needed—good for tracing get-away cars, for finding stolen ones, and for assessing road-usage taxes—but like so many projects of the time, it hadn't come to anything. Majority opinion on the police force blamed the civil-liberties people and their desire to make every cop's day a little bit harder, but a vocal minority insisted that the Taelons had quashed the idea for sinister reasons of their own. Boone wasn't sure which theory he believed.

He printed flimsies of the latest batch of theft reports to hand around at call tonight to the oncoming shift. As the junior captain on the force he had to harass the lieutenants, who had to instruct the sergeants, who had to oversee the patrolmen. Just like the army, only with a different enemy.

The door to his office banged open. Boone looked up.

Captain Delrio swung the door closed hard enough to make the shade rattle.

"Will, congrats."

"Thanks, Marty."

The senior captain—immediately below the police commissioner in the chain of command, and everyone said she had the mayor's ear—sat in the chair in front of the desk. She flicked a strand of her lank blonde hair into place behind her ear and leaned back. "Think you'll be able to replace Carruthers?"

The walls of Boone's new office had pale patches on them from the places where now-retired Captain Vince Carruthers' award plaques and framed citations had hung. There were a lot of patches.

"I'll give it my best shot," Boone said.

"Tell you the truth, Will, when the army handed you to us and said 'give our boy a job,' I was worried that you'd turn out to be an empty suit. But you hit the ground running." She paused and tossed the manila envelope in her left hand onto Boone's desk. It landed with an ominously solid thud. "With the bigger responsibilities come the bigger headaches. Take a look at this."

Boone hooked the envelope closer, slit the top, and pulled out the contents: a pile of papers, standard evidence reports and inventory sheets, investigator's note chips, and a sheaf of photos. The photos showed a crime scene. Tape marked out a section of a field, and in the center of the taped-off square lay a man's body.

"Last night?" Boone asked, flipping through the photos. The corpse was nude. The abdomen and chest were open, cut neatly away in an oval from collarbone to pelvis, and the internal organs were missing.

"No, a month ago," Captain Delrio said. "Not announced until we could inform the next of kin. And here, a month later, we're still running in circles. No next of kin. No idea who the man was at all."

"I suppose you'll be telling me there's no perp, no motive, and no weapon either?"

Captain Delrio gave him a crooked grin. "That's why I promoted you, Will. ESP is a very important quality for a senior officer to have."

"Have you considered running photos of the guy's face in the vids over a 'Have you seen this man?' banner?"

"None of that. Word from the top is that there is to be absolutely no publicity given to this case. Nada, zip, nil."

"The mayor?"

Delrio shook her head. "Higher than that. As in, D. C. There are some real sweethearts back east, let me tell you."

"I know," Boone said. "I used to work for a couple of them."

"Give 'em my best at the class reunions, okay?" Delrio smiled briefly, then went on. "This case is shaping up to be a real mess—when bigwigs from the government start putting on the pressure, it's always a bad sign. It could go sour in a heartbeat and take down the investigating officer with it."

"Ah," said Boone, unsurprised. "Hence the promotion—so whatever happens, at least the Denver PD doesn't lose a senior captain over this one?"

"ESP," Captain Delrio said. She stood and opened the door. The paint on the glass announcing that this space belonged to CAPT. WILLIAM BOONE was still tacky. "I knew I promoted the right man."

She let herself out.

Boone sorted through the papers and disks on the desk after the door closed. He'd check out the contents of the disks and chips in a moment. Right now he was trying to get a feeling for what was there. He closed his eyes. ESP would be really handy.

Then he sighed, opened his eyes, and slid the disk labeled AUTOPSY into the computer drive. Time to start earning that fancy new paycheck.

Some time later, he stood up and stretched. Police work hadn't changed so much with the coming of computers and globals that a good man from Scotland Yard in Queen Victoria's day wouldn't have had his share of successes in the first half of the twenty-first century. After a month there probably wasn't anything worth seeing at the scene of this particular crime, but he wanted to get a feel for the lay of the land. Access, lines of sight, they were all important—and none of them came through in a report.

He shrugged on his sports coat to cover his shoulder rig and the badge that hung from a holder on his belt. Even though he was no longer in the Army, and hadn't been for a couple of years now, he still preferred dark, subdued colors that let him move through the crowded streets without attracting undue attention. Then he walked out through the bullpen, shutting the glass-paned door behind him. The envelope full of evidence was in his right hand.

"Going somewhere?"

The speaker was Bob Morovsky, who until yesterday had been one of Boone's fellow lieutenants. The man had a deeply lined face, as if all the cares of the world rested on him every night. Office betting had been that he would be the one to get the captain's bars next. He didn't look like he was resenting being passed over, though. Maybe he'd already heard some rumors about the gift-wrapped box of trouble that came with the promotion.

"Duty calls," Boone replied. "Anything I need to know?"

"Just planning to invite you and Kate over to my place after work, so we can have a private celebration where the bosses can't see you."

"I may be late," Boone warned him, holding up the manila envelope by way of explanation.

"After twenty years Dot's used to it. Should I warn her?"

"Not telling your spouse everything can get you in a world of hurt."

"Except when telling her everything gets you there," Morovsky said. "What time do you think you can make it?"

"I have to talk with Katie. I'll give you a call when I'm sure."

"I'll get another six-pack on the way home,"

Morovsky said as Boone turned left, out the door and into the hall.

He made his way down to the basement garage where the duty vehicles stood. He thought about taking his own car, so he could head home afterwards without returning to police headquarters, then dismissed the idea. A late night was coming. Without the usual small army of foot cops knocking on doors and asking questions, this investigation would take even longer and have even less of a chance.

As he drove the city vehicle out of the garage, he pulled out his global and called home. Kate answered right up. She must have been outside working in the rose garden—her face was flushed, and she was wearing one of his old uniform shirts thrown around her shoulders over a halter top.

"Hey, babe," she said, when she saw who it was.

Boone laid his global on the car seat beside him so that he could talk and drive at the same time.

"Looks like I'll be working late tonight," he said. "I'll try to let you know when I'm going to be home."

"Do you have to?" But she knew the answer to that already, and her expression was more resigned than plaintive. "I was making a roast, and it'll get all dry."

"We've been invited over to Bob and Dot's," Boone said. "You can get in touch with them and have a party without me, and take the roast along. I'll join you as soon as I can."

* * *

The field where the corpse had been found was well outside of town, though near a major road. Boone parked his car and got out to look over the site.

He wasn't looking at the ground itself, really. The remaining remains, as it were, had only weighed twenty-eight kilos. The reports he'd read told him that there had been no blood on scene, and the photos had confirmed it. That told him that the crime had been perpetrated elsewhere and the body dumped here. The road with its easy access gave him the most likely way that the body had been moved.

He walked out into the field. The site wasn't visible from the road, he discovered, although from the road it looked as if you were able to see the whole field. A trick of topography—the minor humps and hollows of the ground hid the disposal area in plain sight. Whoever had dumped the body knew this spot well.

Boone closed his eyes and tried to get a feel for the layout and the situation. No cop believed the "tips" that came from self-proclaimed psychics—but no good cop discounted his own hunches. Hunches saved cops every day. Maybe what he called a hunch was really part of his head putting together small clues into a pattern, one that was recognizable by the subconscious before the conscious mind ever got to it, but feelings like that had saved his neck more than once in the army.

He let himself soak up the sounds and smells for a minute more, eyes closed, before he took a look around.

The dark wall of the mountains filled the horizon

to the west. Nothing helpful there; the mountains had seen generations come and go, and one murder more or less was nothing to them. But the southwest, now . . . off to the southwest stood one of the Taelons' towers, silhouetted against the setting sun. To the northeast, farther off and glistening wetly, was another of the alien structures, this one clinging like a limpet to the side of a human-built office complex.

The body dumpsite was on a line between the two alien constructions.

"Okay," Boone said to himself. "The *very* highest levels."

—text of message sent by Kate Boone to [DELETED BY ARCHIVE SECURITY], Gaithersburg, Maryland, USA.

You said:

>This week's big news: I'm job-hunting. The Project
>got the official axe last Friday. Not surprising,
>really—there wasn't anybody left from the old
>days but the Octopus, the cleaning lady, and me.
>Trust me, Shrew, you picked the best time to get
>out, right at the peak.

Those were the glory days, all right.

Of course, what I remember most about them is being scared to death and chronically short on sleep. But it didn't matter, because something wonderful and terrible was about to happen, and I was going to be there for it.

But we didn't get cosmic enlightenment, and we didn't get interstellar warfare, either—just a bunch of tall blue star-traveling do-gooders who only want to help out. Like missionaries to the heathen, and the heathen are us. No thank you; I believe I'll stay home for a while and grow my roses.

Which are doing fine, by the way. I stuck with

winter-hardy varieties when I made the new garden, and I haven't lost any yet. Gives me hope for my nurturing abilities. I tell you, the old gang wouldn't recognize me, I've gotten so domestic—next stop kids and a puppy and a white picket fence. Will's been promoted to captain on the police force, so it looks like we'll actually be staying in one place for long enough to give the family thing a serious try.

Don't take so long between letters the next time, okay? Just because I've started morphing into the House and Garden Lady doesn't mean I want to lose touch.

— Shrew

PS: Where's the Octopus going now that his baby's shut down?

NINE

Boone's global chimed as he was heading back into the city. He slid the device open one-handed with a flick of his wrist. A uniformed police sergeant looked back out at him from the global's tiny screen.

"Captain," the sergeant said. "Bunco Squad has something they'd like you to take a look at."

Boone suppressed a sigh. Visions of Kate's pot roast danced through his head. "Will it keep?"

"They're hot onto something," the sergeant said. "It's Omerta working this one, and he said it needed to hit a captain soonest."

"Okay," Boone replied. *I'm the junior captain, so I'm the one who gets to miss supper. Some things never change.* "I'll be there in twenty minutes. Tell Omerta I'll see him in my office."

He slid the screen shut and tucked the global back into his pocket. Then he thought better of it, pulled the global back out, opened the screen, and thumbed the "CALL KATE" button he'd programmed.

"Will?" she said as soon as her picture appeared. The background was the interior of Lieutenant

Morovsky's house. Dot Morovsky was in the picture, but out of focus in the background. "Is anything wrong?"

"Nothing's wrong," Boone said. "But you'd better add at least another forty minutes to my ETA. Something else has come up."

"I understand. Don't worry—hot roast or cold sandwiches, we'll have dinner waiting for you."

"And beer," Bob's voice called from off screen. "Don't forget about the beer."

Kate laughed. "And beer."

"Sounds good to me," Boone said. "See you soon. I'll call again once I'm en route."

"See you," Kate echoed. Then her image faded and the screen darkened to black. Boone closed the global again, and drove the rest of the way to police headquarters without further incident.

Robbery/Homicide occupied the floor above the Bunco office in the police headquarters building, and Boone's new office was off the Robbery/Homicide bullpen. When the elevator door slid open, all the officers on the evening shift, the ones who weren't on the streets, were working at their desks, gathered around with coffee and clipboards in the hall, or writing fast notes on lined paper. Computers hadn't brought about the much-touted "paperless office" when they'd been introduced forty or more years before, and it didn't look like they were going to do it any time soon.

Lieutenant Omerta, a bulky man with an expression that made granite look chatty, leaned against the doorpost of Boone's office. He had a detective's gold shield clipped to his belt, and a tan leather shoulder rig sporting a big wheel gun under his left arm. He wasn't wearing a sports coat.

"What is it, Rog?" Boone asked.

Lieutenant Omerta nodded at the closed door to Boone's office. "Inside," he said.

"Okay." Boone opened his door and ushered the other man in. He closed the door behind them, shutting out the babble of voices from the bullpen outside. "What's up?"

"Unplug your computer," Omerta said. "Turn off your global."

"Say what?"

"Humor me, okay?"

"Okay," Boone said. He slid his global into a desk drawer and pulled his computer's plug from the wall. "Now what?"

"'Now what' is this," Omerta said. "There's a guy out there with his fingers stuck into every signal that goes over the net. He's dirty, he's fixing stuff, he's into everything that communicates by wire, cable, microwave, or fiberoptic, and he's trickier than hell. I want to get him."

"I can see how you'd want that," Boone said mildly. He had no trouble believing Omerta's last statement. The lieutenant was showing all the signs of incipient obsession with his current case. "But do you have enough evidence in hand that you can go to a judge for a warrant?"

Omerta shook his head. "Not yet."

"So you can't get him arrested yet, even if you manage to find him. That's okay, we've got plenty of time . . . meanwhile, what is it that you want me to do?"

"First, don't tell anyone," Omerta said. "This guy is *good*—if you so much as breathe a word about the case within range of something with an audio pickup, he's going to have it."

"I suppose nobody has a voiceprint or an ID photo on record for him?"

"We don't have anything," said Omerta. "If anybody ever preserved our man's likeness for the public record, he's tracked down the data and erased it."

"Or else he's lived his entire life outside the mainstream economy," said Boone. "Which would make him a very slick customer indeed. What can Homicide do to help you with the case?"

"If you can lend me guys, that's super. If not—tell me one thing. You got any strange killings on file up here at Homicide?"

"What do you mean, 'strange'?"

"You'll know 'em when you see 'em," said Omerta. "Something like no one's ever seen before."

Boone thought about the case file and the photos Captain Delrio had brought into his office. Another secret, those, and not his to tell. "Nothing comes immediately to mind," he temporized.

"Sure. Well, if one *does* come to mind, let's get together. My boy is probably involved."

"'Probably' gets us nowhere," Boone said. "I'm not interested in pinning a crime on someone purely in order to get him off the street. What kind of solid evidence do you have?"

Omerta scowled. "Plenty of stuff," he said. "Patterns. Disruptions in communications that tend to make the market move different ways. False signals that don't leave a record anywhere. Forgeries."

"Suspicious stuff," Boone agreed. "But where's the Bunco angle?"

"I got a bunch of looted old ladies," Omerta told him. "That good enough for you?"

"If we can tie it to your guy, yes. Did the money come from them, or from their banks?"

"A little of both."

"Get any federal assistance on the bank end?"

"Nah." Omerta looked disgusted. "I felt 'em out, but they won't come in unless I let 'em take over the whole investigation. What do you think Captain Delrio would have to say about that?"

Boone laughed. "I can see the steam coming out of her ears right now. But you don't mind telling me."

"Nope. Now, here's where you come in. My guy, if it's him, he was talking—writing, really; it was a text message—to one of his cronies just today about a killing he did."

"Got a date, a place, a name?"

"Last month," said Omerta. "Right here in town. I don't know the victim's name, but I got a handle on the perp."

"Tell me about him."

"No one knows enough about him to tell," Omerta said. "We only say 'him' for convenience. Could be a 'her.' Anytime you see something funny in the datafeeds, though, you can bet he's somewhere behind it, raking in a percentage. Manipulating data. Reading your secret files. Like I told you, he's that good."

"You said you had a lead on this killing of mine," Will prompted, before Omerta could circle back yet again to the possibly apocryphal skills of his mysterious criminal. "Tell me more about it."

"The guy calls himself Augur," Omerta said. "He's a real information-crime kingpin. Hard to tell how many people he has working for him, or with him, or anything. First time I spotted him was when the stock market was acting like a carrier wave rather than noise. He was manipulating it, picked up some change there. I expect that his first exploit was the salami-slice attack at the Banco Federale de Credito, but that was out of my jurisdiction. Found it while I was researching where he might have come from."

"How long ago was that?" Boone asked.

"Right after the war. He got big fast, for a shadow."

"Any thought that he might be ex-GI? Learned the trade with Uncle?"

"Could happen. Or with the oppos. Either way we're looking at a young guy, fits the profile."

"Those profiles are going to lead us astray someday," Boone said reflectively. "You still haven't told me where you picked up the intel that he was in on my killing."

"I think I have this Augur's back channel sussed," Omerta said. "He's working on metal phone and power lines, not on the fiber optics. So what's so special about them, I ask myself? So I go looking there for EM band stuff, and find nothing. No overlaid amplitude modulation, no overlaid frequency modulation. But you have to modulate *something* in order to carry information.

"So then I remembered that power has three properties, not two. I put my guys out and check the phase, and bingo, there's something. It's coming right by the filters, straight up the power cords. He's modulating the phase, and he can go anywhere, do anything that way. Sneak in, take over, be anyone anywhere."

"Phase modulation?"

"Yeah. Weird, huh? Ever hear of anything like that?"

"Not lately," Boone said—but an image formed itself unbidden in his mind, a picture of a small truncated pyramid plated in gold and silver, tucked away in a cave high up in the Hindu Kush. That object, whatever it had been, had worked on phase modulation, too. "Does he pass his messages there in the clear?"

"When it isn't machine code, yeah."

"Who does he talk to?" Boone asked.

"I'm still working on that."

Boone nodded. "And you know this is him because—?"

"The guy who's doing the stock thing uses phase modulation, which isn't exactly a common technique in the criminal business. And the guy who said he killed someone was also using phase modulation. So there's your link."

"Good enough," Boone said. "Thanks for the lead—if it turns out to be part of my case, I'll make certain Bunco has a piece of the action. But I have to go talk to some other folks first—check things out—you know the drill."

He left the cube and made his way back out through the bullpen to a pay phone in the hall. At the moment, nobody was standing in front of the phone trying to contact a friend or a lawyer; the hall was effectively deserted. He looked up a number on his global, then punched it into the pay phone. For some things, the relative anonymity of a public voice-line was still the best.

"Four Points Travel," said a voice at the other end. "Can I help you?"

"Yes," he said. "I'd like to buy a round-trip ticket to Washington, D.C."

—text of message sent by Kate Boone to [DELETED BY ARCHIVE SECURITY], Seattle, Washington, USA

I heard from [NAME DELETED] the other day; he said that the Project was finally closing down. No point in looking for anything else, I suppose, so long as you've got Taelons.

[NAME DELETED] said you were going to work—or maybe he said "going back to work"; I'll have to check my files—for the private sector. He sounded a bit surprised. I think he believed that you'd taken root in government service and would have to be removed from the Project with blasting powder, like a stump from a garden.

When he told me you'd taken a V.I.P. job in Seattle with [NAME DELETED], I was pretty surprised myself. Seattle's not exactly right in our backyard, but it's a lot closer than Georgetown.

I haven't done much serious work since I left D.C., except for the odd bit of freelance data-wrangling for small businesses around the Denver area. I think I burned out on the big jobs for a while after the Project. Heaven knows, nothing else is ever going to be quite =that= big again.

It looks like I'm going to be operating out of Denver for the foreseeable future, by the way. Will's been promoted to captain on the local police force, so we're here for the long haul. But I'm not averse to the idea of telecommuting for [NAME DELETED] if something especially challenging comes up, so do keep me in mind.

Best,
K. Boone

TEN

More than two years had passed since the last time that Will Boone had walked through the doors of the Pentagon. On that occasion, he'd come in uniform as a soon-to-be-unemployed Army major. He returned in plainclothes as a police captain, on a quest for information he was sure was going to make some people uncomfortable. He didn't know yet exactly who. That was one of the things he'd traveled to Washington to find out.

He left his rented car in the underground parking garage, and made his way to the nearest entrance. The guard at the desk, confronted with an unknown civilian visitor, looked about as pleased as Boone had expected.

"Sir?"

Boone produced his badge. "Captain Will Boone, Denver Police Department. I'm here to talk with Lieutenant Colonel Menendez. SPECWARCOM G-2. He's expecting me."

"Yes sir," the corporal said. "I'll call his office."

A moment later, after a conversation on a hush-hooded terminal, the corporal said, "An escort will take you to the Colonel's office, sir. Are you carrying any firearms or other weapons?"

"No," Boone said.

"Thank you, sir."

A moment later, a Navy petty officer arrived and said, "This way, sir."

Boone strode along, following the escort to the elevator bank in the basement of the C-ring. The path was the same as the one he'd taken when he'd been summoned to the Pentagon before. Indeed, the office to which he was being led was next door to the one where he'd had the interview with the signal corps officer and the man from the NSA.

Lieutenant Colonel Menendez had a desk decorated with a model tank and an American flag. The in-box was empty, the out-box was full. The colonel was standing with his back to the door, near the spot where the room's window would have been if it had rated a window.

Menendez turned around as the door swung closed. "Will," he said "Take a seat."

Boone's first thought was that Menendez had gained some weight since the last time they'd spoken together, back in India. Well, so had Boone, now that he wasn't living on field rations and no sleep and the constant expectation of attack. Neither man was out of shape, but they were both considerably more solid.

Boone had never seen Menendez with his ribbons before. He wasn't surprised to see that the colonel had been to some interesting places and done some interesting things, if the awards for personal bravery and the unit commendations were anything to go by. Boone kept a similar collection in a shoe box back in Denver.

"I got your call," Menendez said. "How can I help you?"

"You recall back up in the Kush?"

"Yeah. A good time was had by all."

"Do you think those signals you were picking up were Taelon-generated?"

There was a brief pause—so brief that if Boone hadn't been watching for it, he wouldn't have noticed. Enough, though, to let him know that the Taelons were still a subject that made some people nervous.

"What's your interest?" Menendez asked.

"I got a civilian intel job," Boone said. "After I got out." He nodded in the general direction of Menendez's desk. "You seem to have done pretty well for yourself. I wouldn't have thought promotion would go that fast in peacetime."

Menendez didn't respond to the distraction. "What sort of civilian intel job?"

"I'm with the Denver police department. Detective captain now."

"So you said when you called. Is this part of your official duties?"

"Yes, it is."

"I could play the 'need to know' game with you," Menendez said, "but I won't. Tell me what you're working on and I'll see if I can help."

"I know this is irregular," Boone said, "but I'm working on a murder case with a lot of nonstandard parameters. You remember showing me that twonky? I was hoping I could get copies of the photos I took of it that day."

Menendez shook his head. "You've been debriefed, Major. I can't show them to you."

"I took those photos myself. I'm not interested in taking away copies or anything like that—just in refreshing my memory. And I figured you'd know where they are now and how to get them."

"Yes, I do. And you aren't cleared for that." The colonel hadn't taken his own seat. Now he was pacing, hands clasped behind his back. "Sorry, Major."

With a mental shrug, Boone abandoned that line of questioning. If he pushed it any further, Menendez would most likely close up completely. Time to ask something else, like a medic pricking the skin in first one place and then another, looking for a response from the nerves underneath. "Anything you can tell me about our blue friends?"

Menendez halted and looked at him sharply. "Do your superiors know you're here?"

Now that, Boone thought, was a definite twitch. "They know I was assigned to this case."

"In other words," Menendez said, "you're on a fishing expedition without approval. Come back with a warrant, if you can find a judge to issue one."

Boone stood up. "Thank you for your time, Colonel. Would you like to get together after work?"

"I don't think that's possible," Menendez said. "And calling again wouldn't be a very good idea. Good day."

The colonel pressed a button on his desk. The outer door opened and the petty officer who had escorted Boone in took one pace inside.

"See the gentleman out," Menendez said. He turned away again.

Boone walked back to his car slowly, his mind occupied with thoughts of the conversation just past. The interview hadn't netted him a chance to look at the pictures, but that had been a long shot anyway—and there had definitely been something odd about Menendez's reactions.

Still lost in thought, he unlocked the car door and slid inside. As he was placing the key in the slot, something hard and cold poked him in the nape of the neck.

"Don't say a word, don't move," a voice said from the back seat. "Slide over, sir. Don't look at me."

Damn, Boone thought. I'm getting careless in my old age. Too much of that soft civilian living.

He did as the voice directed, still feeling more irritation at himself than fear as he did so. He didn't think that his life was at risk, or at least not immediately. The speaker had addressed him with respect, in spite of having what was undoubtedly the muzzle of a handgun pressed against the back of his neck, and had warned him against turning around. Somebody planning to kill him right away wouldn't have bothered with either the respect or the warning.

The driver's-side door opened again, and another man entered the car. He turned the key that Boone had inserted, and the engine fired to life.

"Look straight ahead," the voice from the back seat said.

"Who are you?"

"We're your friends." The man in the back seat laughed. "You may not believe it now, but it's true."

Boone allowed himself to relax while he sized up the situation. The driver—a bulky, dark-clad shape in his peripheral vision—handled the wheel in a confident manner, rounding the corners, going up toward the entrance to the garage. A security checkpoint with a guard awaited at the top of the ramp.

At that point, Boone thought, he might be able to open the passenger-side door, jump, roll, and escape. The man beside him was big, but both hands were occupied. The man behind him, the one with the handgun, would be hampered by having to have it out of sight while passing by the sentry, and after that the doorpost and the door on the passenger side would block his aim.

The car made the final turn and headed up the ramp. Boone let his eyes find the door handle. He'd make his move at the very top, as the car slowed.

A twist of cord dropped over his head and pressed against Boone's throat. He recognized the move, and the weapon. A garrote.

"Just in case you were planning to make a stupid move, sir," the man in the back seat said. "It's monofilament nylon. Invisible at a couple of feet, but strong enough to take your head off."

"If you're my friends," Boone said, "you sure have a funny way of showing it."

"It's for your own safety, sir."

The guard post was getting near. Boone looked forward. The crossbar was up; the sentry waved them through.

"Now, sir," the man behind him said, "I have to ask you to close your eyes. You'll get lots of answers when we get where we're going."

Boone leaned back and closed his eyes. He felt a blindfold slip around his face and tighten down as his captor tied it behind his head. He tried counting turns in the route the car was taking, but soon lost track, and concentrated instead on the ambient smells and noises, trying to figure out where he was and where they were going. He wondered if he'd recognized the voice of the man in the back seat. The fellow seemed to have a Southern accent, but a faint one, as if he'd been away from Dixie for a long time. One of the two men was wearing aftershave, sandalwood.

The light around the edge of the blindfold went away, and the sound of the tires altered. Boone got the impression that they were inside a tunnel. After several more turns, the pressure on his neck let up, the car stopped, and the door beside him opened.

"Please walk with me, sir," the man said. "Again,

while we are friends, I have to tell you that I'm not the only one here, that the others are armed, and that they will take an attempt by you to run as a gesture of bad faith."

"Who exactly are 'we'?" Boone asked.

The last time I asked somebody that question, he thought, I got handed a plum civilian job in Denver and told "don't call us, we'll call you." I wonder if this is when they ask for a payback.

The reply he got merely served to increase his growing suspicions. "People who think the way you do, sir. Please come with me."

The man helped Boone to his feet and led him by the arm down what was, judging by the echoes of their footsteps, a hallway. They came to a halt, a door swished closed behind them, and the floor moved as the elevator they'd entered descended.

The elevator stopped, bouncing slightly, and the doors opened. Boone's escort guided him out of the elevator and down what sounded like another hall. They came to a halt, and Boone felt hands working at his blindfold. The fabric fell away, leaving Boone blinking at the sudden light.

He stood in a low-ceilinged windowless corridor punctuated at intervals with numbered doors. The floor was tiled in alternating black and green squares, and the walls were painted an unremarkable greenish gray. The whole setup had a government-issue air about it; if Boone had needed to guess its original purpose, he would have pegged it as a converted giant-economy-size fallout shelter from the paranoid days of the previous century.

"I'm very sorry about all this, sir," the man behind him said, and stepped forward to where Boone could see—and recognize—him. By this time, Boone wasn't surprised to encounter another familiar face from the old days with Dog Company in the Hindu Kush.

"Sergeant Birki," he said.

—text of message received by Kate Boone and forwarded with attached commentary to [DELETED BY ARCHIVE SECURITY], Seattle, Washington

>Kind lady:
>We haven't met, but we have a need to speak
>with one another about a subject of interest to a
>mutual acquaintance. Face-to-face or text-only,
>as you prefer, but it should be soon.
>
>If you doubt my bona fides (as well you should;
>this world is full of wicked people) then you can
>ask [NAME DELETED] to verify the signature
>block below.
>
>[SIGNATURE CODE DELETED BY ARCHIVE
>SECURITY]

I found this in my mail queue last night, forwarded from the contact address for a freelance job I did last winter. I don't know who the guy is, or why he wants to get in touch with me . . . but he knows the kind of work I did, and he claims you'll vouch for him, and he doesn't =sound= like a troll or a pervert.

So I guess what I need to know is, is this person for real, or not? And if he =is= real, should I get back in touch with him?

Best,
K. B.

ELEVEN

"I'm very sorry it had to be this way, sir," Birki said. "We hope that the Long Blues aren't listening here. There's no reason to think that they aren't trying. Right now we're in a shielded location, underground."

"I see," Boone said. He nodded at the closed and numbered door to which Birki had led him. "What's in through there?"

"Some more people. We want to talk with you about some things. But first, your word of honor that you'll help us, or at least not hinder us."

"You know I can't do that—not unless I know what you're up to."

"Fighting for mankind," Birki said. "I know that you were recruited, back at the end of the war, but maybe you'd forgotten. You're already one of us, as far as the blue-asses know. We hang, you hang."

That's a cheerful thought, Boon reflected. If I'm going to get in trouble for conspiracy, I'd at least like to have the chance to conspire a bit, first.

"So what am I going to get from you people?" he

asked. "I sure hope you didn't drag me all this way for nothing."

"We'll show you some information. Then you'll give us some answers."

"Maybe. If I can."

"A man can't ask for more than that," Birki said. "Go on in."

Sergeant Birki pushed open the door.

The room beyond was dimly lit, almost cavelike except for a bright desk lamp on a metal table. Boone got the impression of men moving about in the shadows, but they remained indistinct shapes outside of the pool of light. What caught his attention was the pile of folders that lay on the table in the yellow glare of the lamp—old-fashioned manila file folders bulging with papers.

"Using computers isn't safe," Birki said, as if anticipating Boone's unspoken question. "The Taelons' advanced communications technology makes electronic file systems an easy target. Go ahead and look at the folders."

Boone stepped forward into the room. The door eased shut behind him. The brightly lit table drew him forward, like iron to lodestone. A folding metal chair sat beside the table. He pulled out the chair and eased his tall frame into the seat.

On top of the stack of folders lay a stiff new one marked US DEPARTMENT OF THE ARMY, TS NOFORN WINTEL. The folder was thin. Boone unloosed the red string that tied it closed and pulled out a sheaf of photographs. And as he'd more than half expected all along, he found himself looking at his own photographs of the pyramidal gold and silver box that Dog Company had found in a cave high up in the Hindu Kush.

He returned the photos to the folder and set it aside, then pulled the next folder from the stack. This one looked quite a bit older. It was scuffed and dog-eared from years of use, and splotched with a long-dried coffee-ring.

Boone opened the folder and examined its contents. The first sheet was a list of times, places, and numbers from the 1960s. The title at the top of the page said "Cattle Mutilations." The folder also contained several sheets of plastic covered with square pockets. Each pocket held a color slide. Boone was an experienced homicide detective; he could look at the pictures without flinching.

The next folder, equally old and worn, had details of human disappearances, correlated to unexplained lights in the sky, dating to the early nineteenth century—long before the invention of airplanes, let alone the notion of aliens from outer space. A hand-drawn graph showed the disappearances coming in waves: a peak, a valley, and another peak, on a cycle a little over twenty-three years apart.

Boone traced out the cycles from the last entry. The year the Taelons appeared would have come on the top of one of those waves.

So it went, folder after folder. Humans reporting

that they had been kidnapped for odd medical procedures. Stories of ships vanishing in the Bermuda Triangle. Sightings of strange creatures, especially tall, gracile blue creatures.

Boone leaned back, closed his eyes, and pinched the bridge of his nose. He heard a chair scrape across the floor on the other side of the table, then give a metallic creak as it took somebody's weight. When Boone opened his eyes and looked, all he could see above the dazzle of the desk light was a shadowy oval of face topped by the glitter of wire-rimmed eyeglasses.

"Well?" the newcomer said. His voice was deep and gravel-tinged. Boone didn't recognize it.

"What do you want from me?" he asked.

"Nothing in here is more recent than ten years old," said the man with the eyeglasses. "Most of it is much older. All of it was explained away when it was fresh. Swamp gas. Psychotic witnesses. Natural predators. The planet Jupiter.

"We know that you're working on a case that could alert the world to the real menace behind the Taelon presence. Too many people think that the bluies are their friends. There's even a religion or two worshiping them. What we want most right now is hard, solid, *incontrovertible* evidence that the blue-asses are right bastards."

Boone nodded slowly. "And it would help if the evidence were disgusting?"

"Yes," said Eyeglasses. "It would help."

"What would you do with the evidence, if you had it?"

"We have to wake up the president. He's the most deluded of them all."

"And then?" Boone persisted.

"And then we see. Everything and everyone has a vulnerability, if only we can find it. If we devote enough national resources to the project, we can find the Companions' weakness. And *then* we can exploit it."

"I understand," said Boone. He paused for a moment, as if thinking. "How do I contact you?"

"Here's a number." The man pushed a card across the table. It had a global access code handwritten on it. "Call. Don't leave a message. We'll be in touch."

"Just like the old days."

"Just like the old days." The man pushed his chair back, stood and moved back into the shadows.

Boone returned to the first folder. He pulled the pictures of the twonky out of their folder and paged through them a second time. The first ones were his, all right, but near the bottom was another set. These photos weren't from the high frozen peaks of the Hindu Kush, though. They showed the same sort of device—a gold and silver truncated pyramid—but the light in these pictures was greenish, the background a browner rock. The backs of the photos in the second set were stamped PERU.

Boone examined the pictures for a long time. At last he put them all back into the folder, retied the red string, and stood. He accepted the imposition of the blindfold again without complaint, and let Sergeant Birki escort him out of the underground complex.

The sergeant didn't remove Boone's blindfold, or give him back control of the rental car, until they had returned to the D. C. area. Even then, Birki didn't volunteer any information about who they had spoken to or where they had been.

"Drop me off at the nearest Metro stop," was all he said. "Go catch your plane. We'll be in touch."

Boone did as he was told. The earlier moratorium on air travel hadn't lasted more than a few months—just long enough for the governments of the world to decide, or to be told, that the Taelons wouldn't mind if humans wanted to fly from place to place on their overcrowded globe.

In the interim, though, a lot of people had gotten out of the habit of flying, and most of them didn't seem to be getting it back. Boone wasn't sure why. Maybe they were made uneasy by venturing into the edges of what everyone these days increasingly thought of as the Taelons' domain.

In any case, the scarcity of passengers meant that Boone had his choice of an aisle or a window seat on the flight home to Denver, and nobody came to sit in the empty place beside him. He was glad for the peace and quiet in which to think. It had been an interesting morning—but now he had to make sense of it, if he was going to get anywhere on the case.

* * *

The plane trip home, unfortunately, failed to provide Boone with any notable insights, although it did enable him to catch up on lost sleep. He arrived in Denver with a couple of hours still left in the working day, and—since that wasn't long enough to start anything new—decided to fill the time as usefully as possible in cross-checking the information he currently had in hand.

Once back in his office, therefore, he opened up his underdesk safe and pulled out the data disks that Captain Delrio had given him earlier. He opened the first disk and looked at the case file. From the file, he located and printed out the names of the police officers who had signed the witness interview forms. Then, list in hand, he walked down to the squad bay and looked over the duty roster. He was in luck: One of the men on his list, a Sergeant Dubcek, was on duty at the moment.

Boone found the sergeant without undue difficulty. Dubcek had just come back from a foot tour inspecting the bluesuits on patrol, and was now handling some more of the endless departmental paperwork.

Boone approached him politely. "Talk with you, Sergeant?"

Dubcek set the paperwork aside with a look of unconcealed gratitude for the interruption. "Sure, Captain. What's on your mind?"

"You worked a bit on a murder case about a month ago," Boone said.

"Yeah. I worked on a bunch of 'em."

"I'm talking about the big mutilation-murder that's got Delrio sweating. I'm assigned to it now."

The sergeant frowned in thought for a moment, then nodded. "Okay, yeah. I remember that one."

Boone breathed an inward sigh. At least the man remembered the case. "Do you have any gut feelings about it, anything that you didn't want to put in the report because you couldn't back it up? Any hunches?"

"Yeah," the sergeant said. "The bluies did it."

"I can see why you wouldn't say that. Not on paper, at any rate." Boone was careful not to let his face reveal anything about his reactions. Given Dubcek's obvious prejudices, the sergeant might as well have been hand-picked for a case designed to make Taelons look bad. "What was it about the crime scene that gave you that feeling?"

"Well," said Dubcek, after another period of extended thought, "it was mostly the body. It wasn't right somehow."

"Okay," Boone said. "What was it that wasn't right? Did you see something that shouldn't have been there, or *not* see something there that should have been?"

"Nobody saw anything. The whole site was so clean it was unnatural. The real people who do that sort of stuff, they're usually messier."

"How about the personnel at the scene? Was anyone there out of place? Did you know everybody, or were there some new guys in the crowd?"

Yet another long pause for thought. "The guys from the coroner's office. I never saw them before."

"That's good," Boone said. He produced the list he had taken from the case file in his office and laid it out on Dubcek's desk. "How about the names on this list? Is there anyone on here who wasn't at the scene?"

"Him, and him—" Dubcek pointed at the names with a stubby finger. "—and her. Not that I ever saw, anyway."

—text of message sent by Kate Boone to [DELETED BY ARCHIVE SECURITY] at [SUPPRESSED BY MAILER]

I don't know who you are, but [NAME DELETED] vouches for you, more or less. What he actually said was:

>Yes, I can verify that key block for you. The gen-
>tleman in question works under the name of
>Augur. I can't guarantee that his enterprises are
>in all cases entirely legal; but you can rely upon
>his competence if nothing else.

So I'm inclined to give you the benefit of the doubt. Tell me what it is that you want to talk about, first—and who =is= this "mutual acquaintance" that you mentioned?—and we can see how things go from there.

But I don't think face-to-face would be a good idea. For some things, plain text is best.

Kate Boone
[SIGNATURE BLOCK APPENDED]

TWELVE

After his small success with Sergeant Dubcek, the remainder of the afternoon proved considerably less fruitful. Calls to those officers whom the sergeant had identified as not being at the crime scene investigation, even when the records listed them as present, turned up nothing. Lieutenant Brett Cassidy was out in the field on a prolonged investigation; Lieutenant Donnie Acquino had left the force permanently; and Captain Eulalia Brewster-Peck was absent on family leave, preparatory to adopting a mixed-race Sino-Indian war orphan from Kazakhstan.

After the last call turned up dry, Boone decided that he'd done enough for the department for one day even by the standards of a compulsive overachiever. It was time to go home. He made a quick call on his global to Kate—"I'm leaving the office now; I should be home in time for dinner"—and began clearing his desk.

He was closing the last file when a knock sounded at his door—it was Lieutenant Omerta, with a folder full of hardcopy material about the mysterious Augur.

"It took me a while to make the copies," Omerta said. "I had to look around for a scanner that wasn't attached to anything else on the departmental net."

The folder wasn't as fat as Boone had hoped it would be, or as Omerta's concern implied. In some ways, what wasn't included—citizenship records, medical history, encounters with the law—was as telling as anything else. The gentleman had no legal identity or picture ID on file, or if he had, somebody had removed both items; and the crimes to which rumor attached his name had other, likelier names attached to them as well.

"What about your case notes?" Boone asked.

"They're all in here," Omerta said, tapping his forehead. "Nothing's written. He'd get to it somehow, and then we'd lose him."

"I see," said Boone. "Keep me posted verbally, then." He paused, struck by a new idea. "If he's doing data manipulation for our mutilation killer, maybe you could get him on forgery of Denver PD digital watermarks or something."

"He's done a lot worse than that, trust me."

"Maybe," Boone said. "But if it's forgery or nothing, we may have to take what we can get."

* * *

Kate was busy in the kitchen when Boone reached home. He guessed that she was doing some kind of stir-fry tonight, based on the number of plates and saucers already lined up on the counter, each one holding a different chopped vegetable or cubed meat.

During his years in the Army, when he'd never known what time he might get back from the field, she'd become an expert at making dishes that could be prepared up to a certain point—the vegetables diced, the meat sliced thin, the sauce mixed up and waiting—then held indefinitely and finished on a moment's notice. Having him working on this case, it seemed, was bringing back all her old habits.

Boone wondered what would happen to Kate's kitchen repertoire if they started a family and she had to feed the children dinner at a regular time every night. Lots of sandwiches and leftovers in his future, he suspected. He paused in the kitchen doorway and watched her add the diced meat to the big wok. It hit the oil with a fierce sizzle.

"Hunan pork?" he asked.

"More or less," she said. "I've adapted the recipe so many times that I might as well give up and call it Spicy Pork Denver Style."

"It smells good."

"That's the general idea," she said. "You look like you need feeding." She added the chopped vegetables to the wok and smiled at him through the resulting cloud of soy-and-garlic-scented steam. "Remember how you were going to take it easy and slack off once you'd gotten your new job in police work?"

"Well, I *did* try. It's just that this case is one of the ones where I can't relax."

"Ah. One of those." She chivvied the meat and vegetables around in the wok for a few minutes, while the aroma of cooking food grew steadily more tempting, then turned the finished dish out into a serving bowl. "Tell me about it."

"It isn't pretty," he warned her. "Murder never is."

"I'd figured that out. What makes this one different from all the others?"

"It's a mutilation killing," he said. "Captain Delrio thinks there may be Taelons involved—or somebody may want us to think that there are Taelons involved, I'm still not sure which. Lieutenant Omerta, on the other hand, doesn't have any opinions about Taelons one way or the other as far as I can see; all he wants is something nasty he can pin on his target-of-the year and make it stick."

"I thought Lieutenant Omerta worked on frauds and scams, not homicides."

"He does. And it gripes the hell out of him when the D.A. can't get a conviction because the jury doesn't understand paper trails and electronic footprints. So the thought that maybe he can tie Augur to something visual, something with plenty of blood on it—"

"Augur." Kate set the serving dish down on the table next to the rice cooker, then seated herself and waited for Boone to take the other chair. "I've heard that name recently. In a professional capacity, more or less."

Boone felt a moment of disoriented surprise, causing him to sit down with more abruptness than he'd originally intended. He wasn't accustomed to regarding Kate's work as something that might intersect with his own. Data-wrangling was something Kate did and was good at, the way she was good at almost everything she bothered to do—from cooking to growing roses. That the world she worked in had its own gray areas inhabited by shadowy figures of dubious morality was a fact that he preferred not to deal with if he didn't have to.

He bought himself some time by spooning rice and stir-fried pork onto his plate, and squaring up the ends of his chopsticks. It was Kate's emphatic opinion that Western silverware and Eastern cooking made a bad match. Boone couldn't taste the difference himself, but pleasing Kate was the important thing.

"I thought you were doing mostly small-business work these days," he said finally. "This Augur person's supposed to be some kind of information-crime kingpin. Omerta says he's dirty—has his fingers in everything from skimming electronic money to blackmail—"

"I've met Omerta a couple of times," Kate said. "And the man could be wrong, you know. He's not what I'd call the sharpest tack in the detective box."

"Omerta's a good cop. And he's right about one thing: Whether this is a fake job or a cover-up, the bad guys are using the services of a highly skilled data wrangler—and all our sources agree that Augur is first-class."

Kate shook her head. "If Augur really is that good, Will, an ordinary police lieutenant like Omerta wouldn't be able to collect as much as a pixel's worth of evidence. Not unless somebody else has been handing it to him."

"If you say so," Boone said. "But that doesn't necessarily mean Augur isn't guilty as sin. It's more likely to mean that his partners in crime are setting him up to be the fall guy for their whole operation."

There was a momentary pause in the conversation. Then Kate said, slowly, "I've been getting the impression—through channels, you understand, 'friend of a friend' kind of stuff—that Augur may be afraid of something like that."

Boone suppressed a flicker of not-quite-jealousy and concentrated on the fact that Kate had just handed him an unexpected lead. "Afraid enough to think about selling out his buddies before they can hand him over?"

"Maybe. It's hard to tell. I could ask—"

"No," Boone said at once, and more harshly than he'd intended. In a softer voice, he said, "No. The last thing you want to do, if that's the case, is scare him off."

"I wasn't planning to approach anyone directly," Kate said. Her tone was a bit stiff; he'd insulted her skill and intelligence, he supposed, by implying that a high-level data wrangler would ever be anything other than discreet. Then she softened her voice in turn, and smiled at him. "But I could put the word out on the net through my friends and the friends of my friends that if Augur has a story he wants to tell, the Shrew is ready to listen."

"'The Shrew'?"

She blushed. "It's a net handle. From Shakespeare. You know, like Katherine in the play?"

"I know where the nickname comes from," he said. "But I didn't know that you answered to it."

"And *that* tells *me* you never gave in to temptation and peeked into my security file, because I was a good little girl and listed 'The Shrew' right there along with all my other aliases and nicknames."

"When you come right down to it, I don't suppose I had a need to know. It's just as well. If I'd thought I was getting married to a shrew, I might have lost my nerve before the wedding."

"And that would have been a bad thing?"

"Very bad," he said. "Talk to the friends of your friends, Kate . . . but be careful. Given a choice between keeping you and bringing in Augur, I'd rather keep you."

—text of message sent by Kate Boone to [DELETED BY ARCHIVE SECURITY] at [SUPPRESSED BY MAILER]

You said:

>Your former employer speaks of your work most
>admiringly, by the way. Had I known I was
>exchanging messages with the fabulous Shrew,
>I would have attempted something more chal-
>lenging than a simple E-mail for your amuse-
>ment.

I'm glad to hear that [NAME DELETED] vouches for =my= handle and sig block as well. You can't be too careful these days. And it's nice to know that my old boss still thinks highly of me. I think highly of him, too.

But if you're not going to say exactly what you did back when you were working for him—with him? whatever—then I don't think I'm going to explain =my= old job in detail either. I was just one of the data wranglers for the Project, like you were just a contract employee.

Best,
K. Boone
[SIGNATURE BLOCK APPENDED.]

THIRTEEN

The next day, Boone devoted most of his energy to double-checking the rest of the paperwork for the somehow Taelon-connected murder case. The first order of business was a call to Lieutenant Bob Morovsky.

"I have to go see a man about a corpse," Boone said. "Want to come along?"

"After an invitation like that, how could I refuse?"

"I knew I could count on you. Let's hit the road."

"Aren't you going to call the morgue and let them know we're coming?" Morovsky asked a few minutes later, as the two police officers made their way out of the office and down to the headquarters parking lot.

"No," Boone said. "I want to see what we find out if nobody has time to think about their answers first."

"Captain Delrio won't like it if the coroner's office comes to her complaining."

"No, she won't," agreed Boone. "But she'd like it even less if there were irregularities in the case documentation and nobody bothered to check them out. I'll take my chances."

The county morgue was an incongruously bright

and clean building, all white tile and shiny gray metal—almost hospital-like, except that most hospitals, in Boone's experience, were kept uncomfortably warm, and the morgue was distinctly chilly. The other big difference took longer to sink in: All the hospitals Boone had known were busy places, full of hurry and constant motion. This place had, instead, a calm and measured efficiency, an ever-present reminder that the people whom it cared for had no need for hurry any longer.

Boone presented his ID to the clerk at the reception desk. "I need to talk with the resident pathologist about your John Doe #402."

"Just a minute, please." The clerk pressed a button on the desk. A stringy-looking man in a lab coat appeared from the inner office. The clerk waved a hand at Boone and Morovsky. "These two guys say they're from the Denver PD. They want to take a look #402."

"I wasn't the guy who did the postmortem on him," the pathologist said. "I was out that day."

"Good," said Boone. "We can get a second opinion that's unclouded by a previous viewing."

"What do you think I'm going to tell you—'oops, he isn't dead'? Sorry, it doesn't work that way."

Morovsky said, "We just want to look at the body. Can you do that?"

"Yeah, yeah . . . I can do that. Come this way."

They followed the pathologist into an echoing room lined with body-sized lockers like so many filing cabinets. The pathologist pulled out #402.

"There you go," he said, gesturing at the body lying on the steel slab. "One corpse, comma, human, comma, eviscerated. What else do you want to see?"

"Take a good look at the abdominal area," Boone suggested after a moment. "What do you make of it?"

The pathologist moved closer and examined the gaping hollow where the victim's abdominal organs had been. "Extremely interesting," he said. "There are no mesenteries."

"No whats?" Morovsky asked.

"The connective tissue that holds the intestines together in a compact mass." The pathologist regarded the mutilated body with something like disapproval. "Even given the extensive disembowelment we see here, there should have been traces remaining in the corpse of the deceased."

"Any idea why there aren't?"

"I couldn't say."

Boone frowned at the entirely-too-tidy corpse. Something was nagging at him, an impression, perhaps, or a thought engendered by the macabre display. "Check to see if it's human," he said. "I'm beginning to wonder . . . ."

"So am I," said Morovsky. "Where do you get these ideas?"

"Dubcek said the corpse looked too clean to be real," Boone told him. "And it occurs to me that the man had a point."

He turned to the pathologist. "Can you check it for being human?"

"DNA testing can take several days even if it's a

rush job. But if you want something rough and ready—"

"All I need at this point is a yes/no."

"—I could do a blood serum check on the victim."

"Do it," Boone said.

The pathologist busied himself working over the corpse for a few minutes, then vanished back into the farther recesses of the building with a test tube.

"Wait here," he said over his shoulder. "I'll be done shortly."

The time stretched out longer than Boone had expected—there weren't any magazines to read in the body storage locker, and the atmosphere wasn't one that encouraged conversation. When the pathologist returned, his mildly irritated expression had changed to one of genuine disgust.

"I don't know what's going on here," he said. "The serum check doesn't show any human blood at all. Only bovine."

"'Bovine'?" said Morovsky.

"Cow's blood," said Boone. "It's a fake."

* * *

"That was an easy one," Morovsky commented to Boone as they drove back to headquarters from the county morgue. "I don't know how Captain Delrio's going to take it, though."

"That's why she's in charge and I'm not," Boone said. "She gets to be the one who figures out how to tell people that our crime-of-the-century mutilation murder was a high-level hoax."

"Very high level," Morovsky said. "I sure couldn't have told the difference without the test results, and I've seen the real thing more than once."

"Yeah. That's a whole different story—building a fake like that takes some expensive talent, and you have to wonder who was buying it, and why."

Boone parked the car in the departmental parking lot, and the two police officers started back to their offices on the Robbery/Homicide floor. In the elevator halfway up, Boone's global chimed. He pulled it out and slid open the screen. The pathologist from the county morgue looked back at him from the display.

"Captain Boone," the pathologist said, as soon as the image had settled. He looked nervous and upset.

"I'm here."

"Captain Boone—have you made your report yet?"

"Not yet. I was just about to."

"Please don't. At least not in the terms you were probably considering. You have to understand—I redid the serum test, and my initial analysis was seriously in error."

"'In error'—you mean it wasn't cow's blood after all?"

"There *was* cows' blood," said the pathologist. "But there was also human blood, and a closer examination of the corpse at the cellular level shows that the tissues of the body are in fact human as well."

Wonderful, Boone thought. There goes one theory shot to pieces.

"What was all that cow's blood doing in there, then?"

"We speculate, said the pathologist, "that it was added to the corpse either during or immediately after the moment of death, for reasons which we do not yet understand."

In other words, it beats the hell out of you, too.

"Thanks," Boone said. "We appreciate the effort on your part. If you come up with any new theories, don't hesitate to call our number." He slid the global shut again. "And that was our wild goose chase for today," he commented to Morovsky. "Sorry for dragging you along."

Back in his office, Boone started the laborious process of arranging the results of his interviews with Dubcek and the pathologist into an interim report for Captain Delrio. There wasn't much to include. The entire Washington sidetrip, for example, had to be written off as unproductive research—he hadn't found what he was ostensibly looking for, and what he *had* found was too dangerous to tell.

So now he had to think of something, anything, to tell Captain Delrio. "Hell with it," he said at last, and turned to his desk comp with a new resolve.

He was tired of people like Omerta and Sergeant Birki telling him not to use his computer. He was going to use it anyway. And if using it happened to scare something out of the woods—then he'd know what the tiger he was stalking really looked like.

He started a net search on unsolved mutilation murders. A file opened, then another, then more . . . entirely too many hits to deal with effectively. He adjusted the search parameters to cover the United

States only, in the past year only. Fewer files turned up, but there were still a lot. It seemed that despite the coming of the Taelons with their promises of peace and plenty, folks were still chopping one another up on a depressingly regular basis.

He opened a second search: cattle mutilations this time, with the same search parameters. Then he correlated the two searches, looking for those that had happened within a month of each other and within a hundred miles of each other.

The results this time were manageable: only three.

He called up the open files for the first and most recent murder case. The details were nasty. Boone took notes anyway. He printed out witness lists for both the human murder and the mutilations, then got the details on the second and third cases.

When he'd finished, he called Captain Delrio on his global. "That case," he said. "The one you handed to me. It's going to take me out of town for a few days."

"Again?" Delrio looked resigned. "Okay, check in when you get where you're going."

His next call was to the motor pool in the basement garage, for a car. Last, he called Bob Morovsky.

"How'd you like to go for another ride?"

"How far this time?"

"Up to Montana, first. It'll be about a week."

"Montana's a little bit beyond our jurisdiction," Morovsky pointed out.

"Delrio's okayed it special."

Morovsky looked as curious as somebody with his

naturally morose features could manage. "What angle are you working on now?"

"I'll tell you on the way," Boone said. "Maybe nothing."

"One of those cases, is it? I'll tell Dottie, then."

"I'll call Kate. Pack a shirt; see you here in three hours."

"Okay. See you."

Boone swivelled back to his desk and turned to the first witness list. He looked at the photos and reports. Maybe it really *was* nothing. But he'd been playing the intel game long enough to know that a hunch was something other than merely nothing, and that those photos of dead cows he'd been shown back in DC were meant to guide him onto a path.

He punched in the global code on the standard crime report sheet for the sheriff who had filed the cattle report. Jenkins, the man's name was. Sheriff Cliff Jenkins.

When the man's image popped up on the screen, Boone introduced himself and said, "Sheriff, I want to talk with you about some dead cattle. You reported the incident on the fifteenth of last month."

"Damn shame," Jenkins said. He was a lean, graying man, with a bedraggled mustache that looked like he chewed at its drooping ends. "Insurance didn't pay off on it, either. Said it was a lightning strike, and that's an act of God."

"I understand," Boone said. "I was wondering if I could come up there, have a look around, talk with a few folks."

"No need to do that," Jenkins said. "Everything there is to see's in my report. Buried the poor dumb things with a bulldozer."

"Would it be okay to come visit anyway?"

"Don't know why you'd bother."

"Just a couple of questions I want to clear up about a similar case down here," Boone said. "I won't take much of your time."

"Come on up, then. But I can't see how it'll do you any good."

"Thanks."

Boone shut the global, stood, and walked to his window. The lights were coming on in Denver, and the streets below were full of commuters making their way home for the night. Watching them, he felt a sudden wash of envy pulling down on him like a cold undertow, no less strong for being more than half expected.

He sighed, stretched, then opened up his global again and punched the CALL KATE button .

Might as well tell her not to wait up.

—text of message sent by Kate Boone to [DELETED BY ARCHIVE SECURITY], Gaithersburg, Maryland, USA.

You wrote:

>So how's the Home and Garden Lady doing?
>Inquiring minds want to know.

I'm going to get you for that someday, really I am.

The Home and Garden Lady is doing just fine, thank you. The roses are flourishing, I've got enough freelance work to keep from getting bored, and a mysterious stranger who calls himself Augur is sending me messages about setting up a time and place for discussion of a "mutual friend."

And I wanted to ask—you wouldn't by any chance =know= this guy, would you? It's not like you never took a walk on the wild side yourself. You and I both know that the Octopus was bringing in the best he could get and not asking questions, which in some people's cases was a damned good thing. Naming no names, of course.

The Octopus vouches for the identity of this guy's sig, by the way. Not surprising—our old boss knows everybody. But I'd kind of like to know where he knows this particular body =from=. I have my dire suspicions, and they aren't the sort of thing a lowly data wrangler can ask a senior V.I.P. about, especially if she cherishes hope of getting the V.I.P. to throw a freelance job or two in her direction.

Seriously, if you're in trouble with this Augur person, I'll do what I can to help you out, as long as it isn't something that'll get Will into trouble at his job. Police departments have no sense of humor when it comes to data; I have to be even better behaved than I was back when I was an Army wife. Poor me. Such a sacrifice.

If the "mutual friend" =isn't= you, of course, then I've got other worries. And would =definitely= appreciate any info you've got on this guy.

Best,
Shrew

FOURTEEN

The Trail's End Motel in Buffalo Grass, Montana—two hours by road from Bozeman and six hours at least from anyplace else—was a dump. It had cigarette burns on the carpet, sagging mattresses on the narrow twin beds, and a bilious green sign in the shape of a pointing cactus flashing on and off outside the window. The room air smelled of mold and ancient tobacco smoke.

Boone was faintly disgusted with himself for disliking the motel as much as he did. He was going soft, too long away from working in-country and living off what he could carry and the land could provide, if he couldn't appreciate the virtues of a place where the water was hot and the air conditioner was cold and nobody was shooting at him.

The long drive up from Denver had exhausted him without making him sleepy. He'd watched the late news over the room's vid-link—no national interest, as yet, in mysterious mutilation-killings of men and cattle—then left the room briefly to purchase a bottle of cold spring water from the vending machine outside. Now he stood looking out at the darkness through half-drawn curtains, watching the lights of the big trucks as they rumbled past along the highway.

"You think that sign's going to keep on blinking all night?" Bob Morovsky asked, the last few words of his question a stifled yawn. The police lieutenant had already changed from his working clothes into plaid cotton pajamas, and appeared ready to turn in for the evening.

"Probably," Boone said. "They've still got rooms empty."

"If there was any place else to sleep inside a hundred miles," Morovsky said, "they'd still have this one too."

"Yeah, well, there isn't so they don't. It's only for one night. Maybe two."

Morovsky sat down on the twin bed farthest from the window and stretched his pajama-clad legs out on top of the bedspread. He leaned back against the rickety wooden headboard and looked over at Boone for a moment.

"So," he said finally. "Are you going to tell me what this trip is all about?"

"It's kind of complicated."

"So use short words. But I can't work with you if I don't know what's what."

"All right," Boone said. "To begin with, there's that mutilation-murder we've been investigating."

Morovsky shook his head. "Not exactly the rarest thing in the world, I'm sad to say. But why we need to make a road trip to Montana in order to solve it—"

"Bear with me, all right? It's no secret that a lot of people think that the Taelon Companions are somehow involved. And Captain Delrio said that somebody higher up tapped me specifically for the investigation."

"Lucky you."

"Yeah," Boone said. "The thing is, I'd feel a whole lot luckier if I could figure out whether I'm supposed to prove that the Taelons did the killing, or that they didn't."

"They didn't do it."

Boone looked at his partner curiously. "What makes you say that?"

"You've been a cop for two years, Will," Morovsky said. "But me, I've been a cop all my life, and my dad was a cop too. Call it 'cop nose.'"

"Can you explain it any better than that?"

"I'll give it a try," Morovsky said. "Let's say the blue guys actually did it. Okay. They have a hundred million or so square miles of land to dump the body in, and about three times that much ocean. Most of it empty. Not counting outer space and the back side of the moon. So why do they dump the body in the middle of an open field where it's sure to be spotted?"

"Because they flat don't care what people think?"

"No. If the Taelons didn't care about our good opinions, they would have walked in and taken whatever it was they wanted from Earth in the first place, instead of pussyfooting around with good deeds and get-acquainted videos. You and I both know that. Which means that someone else wanted the body found, and wanted the Taelons blamed for it."

Boone nodded slowly. "Well, it's a theory."

"Bet you a fiver it's the right one, too." Morovsky yawned and switched out the bedside light. "Get some sleep, Will. The case will still be there for you in the morning."

* * *

The next morning, after breakfast at a local diner that had been serving fried eggs over easy to ranchers and truck drivers since 4 A.M., Boone and Morovsky went down to the town offices to keep their appointment with the local law. They found Sheriff Jenkins working at a cluttered desk in the room that—according to the building directory—he shared with the state police and the single local police officer.

The office door was open. Boone knocked on the door frame before stepping on through.

"Afternoon, Sheriff," he said. "I'm Captain Boone, from the Denver police department, and this is my partner, Lieutenant Morovsky. We talked yesterday."

Sheriff Jenkins put down his paperwork to look at Boone. His expression wasn't that of a man greeting an expected caller. "We did what?"

"Talked," Will said. "On the global." He was starting to wonder if he'd gotten the right office—or even the right town—but the draggly mustached older man sitting at the desk in front of him looked exactly like the man he'd spoken to yesterday, and he was certain he'd punched in the right number from the report.

Meanwhile, Jenkins was staring at him as if he'd

shown up talking gibberish. "From Denver, you say? Have any ID?"

Boone and Morovsky presented their badges. Jenkins examined them, then gave a reluctant nod. "Looks like you're both Denver cops, all right. But I still don't know what you're doing all the way up here."

"You don't remember getting my call?"

"Nope. Sorry."

"I'm here to ask about a report you filed around a month ago," Boone said. "About some cattle mutilations."

"I don't know who sent you up here, Captain Boone," the sheriff said. "Because I haven't reported any such thing."

Will opened his global and called up a scanned file copy of the original report. He pointed to the scribbled name at the end. "This isn't your signature?"

"It is not." Jenkins was starting to breathe hard through his mustache. "If I wasn't sure you were the real thing, I'd throw you out of here right now."

"There's a list of witnesses on this report," Will said. He was careful not to say *your report*. "Is there a chance I could talk with any of them, since we've come all this way?"

"Sure, you can talk with them," Jenkins said. "Won't help you."

"And could you show us the site where these mutilations supposedly took place?" Boone persisted. "If someone's filing false reports over your name, I suspect that we'd both like to get to the bottom of it. Here's the grid reference."

The sheriff looked at the display on the global, and chewed his mustache thoughtfully for a moment. "That's not too far out of town," he said finally. "And someone put in the names of real folks around here, all right. But it doesn't matter, because none of 'em will tell you anything about something that didn't happen."

The rest of the day involved a lot of driving and a lot of hiking through mud—and worse—in order to talk with people who all said pretty much the same thing: more or less polite versions of "Are you guys crazy?"

As they walked back to their car after the last visit, Will pulled his global and punched in the name of the witness they'd just talked with. A quick search verified that the witness's reported address matched the street sign on the corner where they were standing. He shook his head, and followed Lieutenant Morovsky into Jenkins's marked car.

"Thanks, Sheriff," Will said, when they'd returned to the police station. "Sorry to lead you on a wild goose chase like that. Somebody must have been trying to pull a prank on us."

"Sure looks like that, anyhow," Jenkins agreed. "Don't worry about it too much—things have been pretty quiet around here lately, and it did me good to stretch my legs."

* * *

Back in their hotel room that night, with the air conditioner rattling and wheezing at full blast, Boone and Morovsky popped the tops of a couple of beers from the six-pack they'd scored at an open-all-night convenience store. Boone lay back on his bed and kicked off his shoes, then took a pull of his beer.

"Today was certainly interesting," he said.

"I'd call it pretty worthless, myself," Morovsky said.

"I don't know." Boone took another long drink of beer. It wasn't particularly good beer, but it was cold, and he'd drunk worse stuff in stranger places than this. "Do you think Jenkins showed us the right field?"

Morovsky shrugged. "The grid posits matched."

"That doesn't mean anything. I can't tell one square mile of farmland—"

"Ranch land. It's all ranches, around here."

"—of ranch land from another. We could have been over the hill from the right spot and never even known it. The photos in the report showed a couple of broken fenceposts."

Morovsky's expression sharpened. "The fenceposts in the field we looked at had been standing there for years. The barbed wire was rusted onto them."

"So you noticed that, too," Will said. "I thought you had. And Jenkins was right, the supposed witnesses all denied ever seeing or saying any such things."

"Which leaves us—where?"

"Which leaves us moving right into info-war territory."

"You make that sound like a *good* thing," Morovsky said.

"I wouldn't call it exactly good. But it does let me get a grip on what may be going on."

"Enlighten me," Morovsky said. "Pretend that I don't know diddly."

"I'll give it a try . . . as you know, Bob, I talked to this Jenkins person on the global yesterday. Same guy, all the way down to the crumb-strainer mustache. He had a different story then. Faking a global call in real time can be done—Kate could handle it if she wanted to, I think—"

"'Kate'? *Your* Kate?"

"She doesn't just grow roses," Boone said. "Which reminds me, I need to call her and let her know we'll be out in the field for another couple of days. Anyhow—faking a live global conversation in real time takes high-level data and image manipulation skills. And then there are the police reports."

"Which we know have to be fake."

"Which are a good bet to be fake, anyhow. I suppose that somebody could have hired actors to impersonate Sheriff Jenkins and a bunch of local ranchers for the duration of our visit, and run the fake that way, but I don't think so. Too many people involved, too short a time to set it up in—"

"Too expensive," contributed Morovsky. "Out-of-work actors good enough to look convincing aren't as cheap as you think they'd be. And that doesn't count the expense of having to pay out hush money afterward. I've seen the results, and they're not pretty."

"You'll have to tell me more about that case sometime," Boone said. "But the principle holds: Working with data is cheaper and cleaner than working with people. Even though blank police report forms are all crypto-stamped these days, which makes them damned hard to forge. Something good enough to pass an eyeball test is still going to alert a department scanner during the imaging process."

"But you called up all those reports and images two or three times each—"

"And never even got a peep out of the security checkers," Boone finished for him.

Morovsky nodded slowly. "Uh-huh. I think I see where you're going with this."

"Right," said Boone. He finished off his beer and tossed the empty into the trash. "I think that we're getting lied to by experts—and that's always a good sign you're getting close to something that people don't want you to know."

"I'll buy that. So where are we going tomorrow?"

"To the next crime scene," Boone said. He smiled. "This one has some particularly nice features. Including a witness who saw a Taelon there."

"Hallucinating, do you think?"

"We'll see. But you know what? This time I'm not going to call in advance. Let's sniff around on our own before anyone knows we're in town."

—text of message sent by Kate Boone to [DELETED BY ARCHIVE SECURITY], Gaithersburg, Maryland, U.S.A.

You said:

> >No, I'm not "in trouble with this Augur person"—
> >and besides, I don't do that sort of thing any-
> >more either. If I were you, I'd start looking for
> >mutual friends somewhere closer to home.
> >Wasn't your husband up to his eyeballs in the
> >serious spook stuff, back in the bad old days
> >before the Taelons came to show us all how to
> >be peaceful and civilized?

Never mind what my husband did or didn't do. He's a police officer now, and =very= well behaved.

But you've got a point, unfortunately, because I can't imagine who else Augur might be talking about. Not the garden club, surely; and while I can imagine one or another of my local employers stumbling onto something too big to handle, I can't imagine the Cripple Creek Theatre Company or the Fresh Air Decorative Service getting involved in something big enough to involve a man whose sig block is in the Octopus's personal authentication file.

All this is the long way around to saying that you're probably right, and this is tied in with whatever Will is up to at work. It's a first for me, though; his stuff and my stuff never used to intersect back in the olden days. So I could pretend that he was nothing more than an ordinary foot soldier, and he could pretend that I was a nice girl who liked cooking and gardening and happened to work with computers on the side.

That's an awful lot of make-believe, right there—but hey, it worked fine for =years=.

Best,
Shrew

FIFTEEN

The next morning Boone and Morovsky set out on the road again. They ate breakfast at the same diner as the day before. This time Boone had the trucker's special—two eggs any style, hash brown potatoes, and a strip steak. He figured that the special was adding a week's supply of cholesterol to his bloodstream with every bite he took—anything tasting that good had to be bad for you—but he decided that he didn't care. He and Morovsky were looking at another long day full of driving and legwork, with who knew what chance of stopping for lunch, and he needed all the fuel he could take in.

After breakfast the flat road stretched out before them from Buffalo Grass eastward toward North Dakota. The car radio only had three stations in range—a Top-40 station playing the same endlessly cycling lineup of tunes as its equivalent back in Denver; a classical music station on day two of a round-the-clock Telemann marathon; and a station belonging to a religious organization that billed itself as the First Church of the Taelon Covenant. After the third straight hour of baroque harpsichord music, Morovsky and Boone switched off the radio and passed the time in talk.

The conversation kept circling back to the Taelons. Morovsky had already been a Denver cop for ten years at the time when the first images and messages from the alien visitors appeared on the open airwaves. Boone—who had been incommunicado somewhere between central China and India's northwest frontier at the time—found his partner's account of the Arrival fascinating, in a morbid sort of way.

"And nobody even tried to launch a missile or scramble fighter craft or anything?" Boone shook his head. "I'd never believe it if I didn't already know that it really happened that way."

"Everybody was waiting for somebody else to throw the first punch, I guess," said Morovsky. "So in the end nobody did."

"Maybe," said Boone. He thought about Kate's letters, written while she was in Washington working on the Project. "Or maybe the fix was in a long time before most of us ever saw a Taelon, in the flesh or on film."

"Better be careful there. Those are serious burn-your-brain-cells-after-thinking-them ideas that you're working with, my friend."

It was midafternoon by the time the two police officers reached their destination. Tucker's Prairie made the previous night's stop look like a booming metropolis. Buffalo Grass, Montana, had at least still possessed a highway junction to keep it alive; Tucker's Prairie had been dying ever since the railroad left town.

"Are we going to look at the human murder first," Morovsky asked, "or the cattle?"

"The cattle," Boone said. "But before we do *that*, we're going to interview our witness who claims to have spotted a Taelon. With any luck, she won't be a schizo."

"Double or nothing she is."

"Pessimist," Boone said. He consulted his notes and the street directory on his global. "We're looking for one-twenty-seven Union Street."

"Where's that?"

"About three blocks this way, then hang a right. Not the best part of town, apparently."

The house, when they got there, proved to be a single-story frame building with a general air of "waiting to be foreclosed" hanging about it: dull green paint that was years past needing a new coat, sagging front steps, and a roof marred by sad patches of loose shingles.

"What did I tell you," Morovsky said, as they parked the car and walked up to the front door. "Schizo."

"We don't get to choose 'em," Boone said, and knocked.

If the picture in the police report wasn't a lie, the woman who answered the door was the Clara Grigsby who'd been listed as a witness to the cattle mutilation case. She wore a faded gray sweatsuit and a pair of off-brand athletic shoes with no socks, and her mouse-colored hair was pulled back from her face with a plain rubber band.

"Good morning, ma'am," Boone said, flipping open his badge case. "I'm Detective Boone, and this is Detective Morovsky. We'd like to ask you a few questions about the events of the night of last June 21."

The woman looked at them suspiciously from under low eyebrows. "Am I in some kind of trouble?"

"No, no," Boone reassured her. "You're not in trouble. May we come in?"

"Just stand there on the porch," she said. "My housekeeping's terrible. I'd die of mortification. Now ask your questions."

"Ma'am," Boone said, switching his global to record, "Could you tell us about what you saw on the night that you reported seeing a Taelon Companion?"

"I *did* see one," Clara Grigsby said. "Big as life and just like the pictures. Out east of town by the railroad crossing, not a hundred feet from where they found those poor dead cows the next day."

"And what time of day or night was that?"

Another suspicious look, "Don't you have that stuff all wrote down already?"

"Some of it, ma'am," Boone said. "But we'd like to hear it from you. Sometimes reports have mistakes in them."

"Uh-huh," she said. There was a sullen pause.

Boone waited. Finally she said, "It was two, maybe two-thirty in the morning. Like I told them before."

"How did you fix the time?"

"Say what?"

"How did you know what time it was?"

She tapped her forehead. "I know things like that. They come to me."

"Okay," Boone said. Something was coming to him, too: the distinct feeling that he'd be paying off his bet to Morovsky by sunset. "Would you mind riding with us down to the crossing and showing us where you saw the Taelon?"

"I'm not getting arrested or anything, am I?"

"No," said Boone. "But you will be giving a great deal of help to the investigation."

"You'll tell them that down at the police station? That I was a great deal of help?"

"Yes, ma'am," said Morovsky. "We'll tell them."

"Then I'll come."

* * *

Two hours later, Boone and Morovsky dropped Clara Grigsby back at her house on Union Street, leaving her with a business card and a request that she call them if she remembered anything else. Then they drove back, toward the highway, with Boone's global unfolded on the front seat between them, replaying the interview just past. Periodically Boone would halt the playback so that the two police officers could discuss and annotate the record.

Images of warehouses and railroad tracks flashed by on the global's tiny video screen, and Clara Grigsby's voice droned on through the device's tiny speakers:

"I was out by the railroad tracks that night, right around those old warehouses—"

Boone's voice over the speakers said, *"Do you know if the warehouses are currently in use?"*

"No. No, they aren't being used, I mean. They're all falling down now, ever since the railway pulled out and left nothing here for anybody but the weeds."

"If you ask me," Morovsky commented during a pause in the playback, "our friend Clara was out there that night by the warehouses checking on some weeds of her own."

"Maybe," Boone said. "But I didn't see anything—"

"There probably *isn't* anything, by now."

"—and anyway, it's a local matter."

The global's video screen showed another shot of the railroad tracks, and Clara's voice went on: *"I was standing right there when I saw it."*

"The Taelon, you mean, ma'am?" That was Morovsky, sounding patient.

"No. That came later. First thing I saw was the ship. It was a great big light in the sky, and it moved without making a sound, except for a kind of a whoosh and a bang when it first showed up. I'd never have seen it, maybe, except for that first noise."

"Maybe she wasn't inspecting her weed garden,"

Boone interrupted, pausing the playback again. "Maybe she was meeting her boyfriend out there."

Morovsky shook his head. "I don't think so. She doesn't look like somebody who's got a boyfriend."

Boone restarted the playback. *"What made you realize that this light was actually a spacecraft?"*

"It had lights all around, but not the usual lights you'd see on an airplane. And it moved wrong. It went off in that direction"—the Clara on the global screen pointed off to her right—*"and then it vanished. I think it landed somewhere out of sight."*

"Did you think about the Taelons then?"

"I thought I wanted to go see. So I started walking."

"And we didn't find her footprints, or anybody else's, either," Morovsky said. "No physical evidence to show that she's ever been down that way at all."

"Maybe not," Boone said. "But did you catch a good look at her eyes while she was telling us the story? Her pupils got wider, and her nostrils were flaring. Something she saw back there scared her, and she's still scared."

He started the playback again. *"You started walking."* His voice over the global sounded easy and soothing. *"Then what happened?"*

"Then I felt something touch me on my shoulder, like a hand, and I turned around, and—you're not going to report all of this, are you?"

"No," Boone said. *"Not if you don't want us to. Just tell us what happened."*

"I . . . I wet myself," Clara said. *"Peed right in my pants. Don't tell anyone."*

"Not a word," Morovsky said. *"Unless it's really important. What did you see when you turned around?"*

"I don't know if it's important or not . . . except that what I saw was a Taelon, up close. Blue, and tall, and dressed up in one of those spangly body suits like they wear on the TV news."

"Did the creature attempt to communicate with you?"

"It sort of hissed at me. There were words, but I couldn't make sense out of them. They weren't in English, or in Spanish either—I had a year of Spanish in high school, you know? Then I felt a cold patch on my arm, and the next thing I knew I was waking up inside the alien's ship."

Morovsky asked, *"How do you know that's where you were?"*

"Where else could it be? It was all full of bright lights and metal and stuff. And that Taelon. I couldn't move, and I couldn't see what it was doing to me, but I know that it was something nasty, if you know what I mean."

"I'm afraid I don't know what you mean," Boone said. *"Could you be a little more specific?"*

"I mean it was doing experiments. Like a doctor would, only it wasn't any doctor. Then I passed out again, and when I woke up I was back at my house. They found those cattle the very next morning."

Boone switched off the playback on the global. The rest of the story was a simple one: Clara told a couple of friends about her scary experience, and they told other friends, and one thing led to another. Pretty soon the local town police arrived, asked Clara some questions, and left. And that was the last she had heard of the incident until the two big-city cops had turned up on her front porch.

"So what do *you* think of her story?" Morovsky asked Boone, after the playback had been turned off.

"I think that I want to take a closer look at those abandoned warehouses," Boone said. "There's something not quite right about them."

"Okay. Think we should get a warrant?"

"For what? This isn't a search. It's just an informal lookaround."

"We don't want to have the whole case thrown out of court later, though."

"I wouldn't worry about it too hard," said Boone. "Anyone who presents Clara as a witness is going to lose their case anyway. And there's no precedent for trying a Taelon."

"I told you back two nights ago that the Taelons aren't involved in this."

Boone shook his head. "That's the Denver case. Here we have a witness who puts a Taelon on the scene."

"Yeah, but the scene of what?"

"It's the same MO as our case. Those cattle weren't simply killed: they were hollowed out, same clean lines, same everything, exactly like my corpse back in Denver. That's a pretty good correlation."

They pulled the car up to the row of warehouses, and Boone got out. "I saw something out here that I didn't want to get into with Clara along," he said over his shoulder to Morovsky. "These warehouses are supposed to all be abandoned and falling apart, right?"

"Right."

"So what's behind that door over there with a brand-new padlock on it? I'm going to guess—and my guess is that what's inside that warehouse is a room that looks like the inside of a flying saucer."

—text of message sent by Kate Boone to [DELETED BY ARCHIVE SECURITY] at [SUPPRESSED BY MAILER]

Enough of this dancing around. We might as well get down to specifics. What exactly is it that you need to discuss with me—and what is it that you want me to do?

Shrew
[SIGNATURE BLOCK APPENDED]

SIXTEEN

Picking the lock on the deserted warehouse didn't give Boone any problems. He was glad to see that he hadn't lost the touch since his time in the field with Special Operations.

Morovsky was impressed, though. "You cracked that one like a professional."

"Expensive government training," Boone said. "You wondered where your tax dollars went to—well, that's the answer."

"I suppose you've sworn to use this power only for good."

"Something like that, anyhow."

Boone gave the unlocked door a gentle push, and it swung open. The two cops entered the warehouse carefully, Boone first and Morovsky a pace or so later—not drawing their weapons, since there wasn't any immediate threat, but leaving each other with clear fields of fire just in case.

The warehouse was empty. Boone hadn't been joking, or at least not much, when he said that he expected to find a Taelon spaceship stage set inside, but all a swift first glance could show him was a bare concrete floor and bare walls.

"Looks like you rolled snake-eyes this time," Morovsky said.

"Maybe." Boone pulled the mini-flashlight out of his jacket pocket and used it to look more closely at the floor. "See the scrape marks there, and there, and over there?—somebody's been moving large objects in and out of here."

"It's a warehouse," Morovsky pointed out. "Holding large objects is what it's for."

"The railroad hasn't passed through this town for at least two decades," Boone said. "And there hasn't been any local industry in Tucker's Prairie for almost as long. These marks are all new—newer than that, anyhow."

"And you think the stuff involved was the bits and pieces of your Taelon spaceship."

"I think it could have been." Boone was shining his mini-flashlight into the corners of the warehouse as he spoke, and along the edges of the floor. The beam of light touched briefly on something lighter in color than the surrounding concrete. He halted and swung the flashlight back.

"I think we've got something," he said. He strode over to check out the unknown object, then beckoned to Morovsky. "Hey, Bob—come take a look at this."

Seen up close, the item in the beam of the flashlight was easy to identify: a bald-head wig, of the kind an actor in a stage drama would wear. But this headpiece, done in pale blue-tinged latex and equipped with built-in elongated earlobes, could only have been designed for a single role.

"I think we've found Clara Grigsby's Taelon," Boone said. "What's left of him, anyway."

"It's not going to do you much good in court," Morovsky said. "I don't have a warrant—*you* don't have a warrant—can you say 'illegal search and seizure'?"

"Maybe not—there's all kinds of exceptions to that rule. Remember the Patty Hearst trial?"

"That one was quite a bit before my time. Quite a bit before your time, too, unless you've been using some really good hair dye."

"They taught us all about it in the service," Boone said. "Under the rules of search and seizure. One of the documents in the case came from a search of Bill and Emily Harris's house. It was a bad search, even for the way they did things back then—no warrant, no probable cause, just kicking in the door—and it didn't produce anything that could be used at the Harris' trial, because their rights had been violated all to hell. But that same document—'Tanya's Diary'—was perfectly admissible at Patty's trial, because she didn't have any reasonable expectation of privacy in somebody else's home."

"So we officially don't care if the owner of this warehouse avoids any legal consequences."

"My guess is that the owner of this warehouse

doesn't have the foggiest idea about what's been going on in here. But the people who used this space, with or without the owner's permission—they don't have any right to expect us not to come in here and look around. So here we are, and what we find, we find."

"If you get this case thrown out of court," Morovsky said, "Captain Delrio is not going to be happy."

"I'm not sure this case is even supposed to get to court," Boone said.

"One of *those* cases," said Morovsky. "Wonderful."

"Yeah. But we do what we can. Let's go."

The two cops left the warehouse, closing and relocking the door behind them. Their car was still parked where they had left it. Morovsky tossed the evidence bag into the back seat and Boone slid behind the wheel. The sun had gone down while they were inspecting the warehouse, and the night was getting dark. Overhead against the star field, one moving star—a satellite making its nightly pass—swept across the sky from north to south.

"Getting late," Boone said. "We'll see what kind of night-duty judge the locals have on tap."

Morovsky reached for his global. "Want me to call it in? A town this small, we may have to go all the way to the county seat to find a judge."

"No, let's do this face-to-face," Boone said. "If someone's playing games, we'll give them one less round."

"Any reason to think that the bad guys—whoever

they are—haven't been watching that warehouse all along?"

"Any particular reason you're asking?" Boone asked, his voice carefully neutral.

"We've picked up a set of headlights behind us. Pulling in off the side road to the left."

Boone checked the rearview mirror. There were the headlights, just as Morovsky had described them. They looked high enough off the road to belong to a sport-utility vehicle or a pickup truck. "Some farmer on his way into town?"

"Yeah, could be."

Boone kept on driving. Behind them, the other vehicle continued to put on speed. At this rate, it would overtake them before much longer.

"He's sure in a hurry," Morovsky commented. "I don't think I'm going to put any money on it being a farmer."

"Good idea." Boone glanced again at the headlights behind them. Much closer, and the vehicle would come into range to do any number of unpleasant things. "Call up a local map. How far out of town are we?"

"Looks like about twenty miles."

"That's what I was afraid of. You know, that idea about calling in? It sounds a lot better now."

"I was about to say the same thing. Let's see . . . ." Morovsky played with his global for a bit, punching in directories. "Damn," he said finally. "This one-horse town is also a one-cop town, and he's gone to bed."

"What about the Staties?"

"They're a long way off."

By now, the truck behind them had approached to within fifty feet, and a light twinkled beside its passenger-side window. The police vehicle's rear window broke into a pattern of spiderwebbed cracks—the mark of a bullet striking glass.

"They're shooting at us," Boone said. "That's no farmer. Bounce the local guy out of the sack, get some others started. I'll see if I can lose this one."

Boone pressed down on the accelerator. The vehicle's powerful police engine roared and shot them forward. The road stretched out ahead of them, long, straight, and unlit.

"This terrain doesn't exactly present us with a cornucopia of opportunities," Boone said. "Now, if we could make a lot of left turns across traffic . . ."

"If we were somewhere that had traffic, we wouldn't have the same problems." Morovsky was busily punching codes into his global, trying to raise the more distant but active law enforcement. He identified himself, gave his position, and asked for an assist.

"Coming up fast," Boone said. "Let's see what kind of engine they've got."

He stamped on the accelerator, hard. The telephone poles blurred into an oversized picket fence, and the white dashes marking the middle of the road turned from a dotted line to a single continuous stripe. The trailing vehicle fell behind for a few moments, then ceased its backward drift and once again kept pace with Boone and Morovsky—and not far enough behind.

"And the answer is, they've got a good enough engine to chase us until the tank runs dry," Boone said. "Bob, you have a weapon on you?"

"You know I do."

"Then let's make sure that we get out of this alive, okay?"

"Fine by me. Our friends in the state police say that we're pretty much on our own. It'll take 'em a while to get somebody out here."

"Keep them posted. At least there's only one of the bad guys on our tail." Boone drove on in silence for a few minutes, his attention divided between the empty road stretching out ahead of him and the headlights of the pursuing vehicle in his rearview mirror. "Junction with the state highway coming up, hold on for the curve."

"Will," said Morovsky tensely. "There's an *aircraft* up there."

"You'll have to keep an eye on it for me," Boone said. He could feel the tires on the car vibrating. One of them was out of balance. "I'm too busy to look."

"This aircraft, Will—it doesn't have standard running lights. And it's big."

"Like what Clara was talking about?"

"Yeah. Like that."

"Maybe these guys really do have some tall blue friends," Boone said. He took the exit for the highway junction without decelerating, and the car slewed around the curve of the on-ramp in a wail of brakes and a cloud of rubber smoke. Boone accelerated some more.

"Slow down!" Morovsky shouted. "Roadblock!"

"I see it."

A police cruiser, its blue light flashing, was parked across the center line of the state highway. Boone pressed down hard on the brake. The unmarked police vehicle screeched to a neck-snapping stop.

"Out of the car," came a voice from the night, over near the roadblock. "Keep your hands where I can see them."

Beyond the police cruiser the aircraft was settling earthward. It was an ordinary helicopter with a searchlight.

"Oh, well," Morovsky said. He pulled out his gold detective's badge and held it high overhead in his right hand as he exited the car. Boone did the same on the other side.

"Lie down on the pavement," the voice said. "Do it now."

"We're police," Boone shouted, but he followed orders all the same. People can get hurt through misunderstandings, and his pride wasn't so tender that it wouldn't survive the experience.

A uniformed officer stepped forward out of the glare of the chopper's searchlight. "The helicopter clocked you doing over a hundred."

"We were being pursued," Boone said, from the pavement.

"The guys in the helicopter don't report seeing any pursuing vehicle."

"Take a look at our rear window," Boone suggested. "Somebody was shooting at us."

There was the creak of shoe leather as the police officer walked around to the rear of the car and then back again. "Those could be old marks."

"That car came from the Denver PD motor pool," said Morovsky. "Think they'd let it off the lot with holes like that in it?"

"You've got a point," said the police officer. "And your IDs check out. You guys might as well get up, and we'll go straighten out the paperwork back in town."

Boone got carefully to his feet, brushing sand and gravel off of his jacket and trousers, and put his badge away. "If Tucker's Prairie has a diner that serves good coffee and stays open after sunset, then I vote we go straighten out the paperwork there."

* * *

Over coffee and doughnuts at the only late-night diner in Tucker's Prairie, Boone and Morovsky and the representatives of local law enforcement went over the inevitable paperwork. The helicopter, or at least the helicopter that had landed on the highway at the end of the chase, belonged to the state police. The Staties insisted that they had seen no pursuing car; the local cops, on the other hand, were willing to let the fresh bullet hole in the rear window serve as a mute witness to the contrary.

Neither the state police nor the Tucker's Prairie Police Department, however, claimed knowledge of the existence of the bald-head wig. At the start of the car chase, the plastic evidence bag containing the latex wig had been lying on the back seat of the Denver PD vehicle; but when Boone got up from his prone position on the highway and went back over to the car, a quick glance into the rear of the vehicle was enough to let him know that the bag was gone.

"You'll let us know if you get any more mysterious sightings," Boone said later, after fresh-brewed coffee and honey-glazed doughnuts had done their usual job of restoring camaraderie. The subject of the missing evidence bag had been tactfully dropped from the discussion, along with the missing search warrant for the empty warehouse. "Bright lights in the sky, blue aliens, anything like that."

"Sure thing," the local police officer said, and the Staties nodded agreement.

Later, as Boone and Morovsky walked back to their car, Morovsky said, "You know they won't tell us a damned thing."

"Probably not," said Boone, resigned. "But at least we didn't have to contact Captain Delrio and ask her to bail us out of jail."

"Be grateful," advised Morovsky. "The experience isn't one most people would care to repeat."

"Speaking from personal knowledge, are we?"

"Let me tell you about that case someday . . . is that your global signaling, or mine?"

"Mine." Boone slid into the driver's seat of the vehicle, closed the door, and popped the global. The first thing to come up was a still shot of Captain Delrio. Boone put his thumb on the MUTE button and said, "I think we relaxed a bit too soon. She doesn't look happy."

As soon as he hit ACKNOWLEDGE and released the MUTE, Delrio began speaking. "I don't know whose toes you boys have been stepping on," she said. "But I want both of you back in Denver by eight o'clock tomorrow morning."

—text of message sent by Kate Boone to [DELETED BY ARCHIVE SECURITY] at [SUPPRESSED BY MAILER]

You said:

>Events are moving too fast for us, kind lady.
>We could spend weeks upon weeks authenticat-
>ing one another and come no nearer to reaching
>a firm ground for trust. Meanwhile, those who
>wish me ill are acting in the real world, and act-
>ing at speed. As are, kind lady, the ones who
>seek to embroil your husband in this affair.

If you'd done your homework properly to start with, you'd know that my husband has his job and I have mine, and the two don't mix. But you opened this can of worms—was it because you weren't clean enough to talk directly to a cop? I'll bet it was—and now they're squirming all over your keyboard.

If you want to take this any further, we're going to have to meet face-to-face and I'm going to have to see hardcopy and solid media. No more dancing around with this flickering-pixel stuff.

I'll be in the Museum of Natural History this afternoon at three, outside the planetarium. You'll

recognize me, I'm sure—I won't insult your abilities by thinking that you can't find a photo of me archived somewhere for ID purposes.

But I'll be wearing a red rose, just in case the picture was an old one.

Kate Boone
[SIGNATURE BLOCK APPENDED]

SEVENTEEN

It took driving all night to do it, but Boone and Morovsky made it back to Denver by morning. They turned the vehicle back into the departmental motor pool, where the bullet hole in the rear window failed to excite comment—such things happened, from time to time—and took the elevator up to Robbery/Homicide. With any luck, Boone thought, the office coffee urn wouldn't be empty yet, and he and Morovsky would have a chance to caffeinate themselves into a semblance of efficient humanity before taking on a full day's work.

Luck, it developed, was not on their side. The first person they met, out in the bullpen, was Sergeant Dubcek, and he had a message to deliver.

"Hey, Boone," he said. "The Captain's been looking for you, and boy, is she hot. In her office, pal."

Morovsky shook his head. "Better you than me."

"Save me a doughnut and a cup of coffee," Boone said. "I'll need them after this is over."

He took the stairs up to Delrio's office, not waiting for the elevator. The office had its door standing open, and Boone could hear her talking to someone as he walked down the hall. The conversation sounded one-sided: a global or telephone conference, then, not a face-to-face.

"Boone, come in, shut it behind you," she said as Will knocked at the door frame. Captain Delrio was standing at her office window—she was senior enough to rate an office with a view, even if it did look out eastward over the flat country and not west toward the mountains. She had her global in one hand, and slid the device closed as she spoke. "Captain Boone, you are in a world of trouble. You know how that case you were working on was supposed to be kept quiet? Well, the word's gotten out."

Boone hadn't heard—he and Morovsky had kept the car radio tuned to the First Church of the Taelon Covenant for the whole ride home, letting its high irritation value keep them awake when coffee and conversation failed to do the job—but he wasn't surprised. He'd never seen a civilian yet who could keep a secret, and from the point of view of Special Operations, even cops were civilians.

"Gotten out where and how?" he asked.

Captain Delrio refused to be sidetracked. "You tell me first that the leak didn't come from our side."

"If it's any consolation," Boone said, "it probably didn't. Remember—there's someone else out there besides us who knows all of the gory details. The perps know what's going on; they could have let the word slip out."

"The Taelons aren't stupid enough to—"

"No, Captain," Will said. "I don't think the Taelons had anything to do with this murder."

"Do not interrupt me," Delrio said. "One way or another, the Taelons are involved in this up to their skinny blue necks. Have you seen the news vids this morning?"

"No. We drove straight through."

"There are anti-Taelon demonstrations breaking out all over the country—people in the streets protesting against unsolved murder cases just like this one."

"I hadn't heard about the demonstrations," Boone said, "but I should have expected something like that." In a perverse sort of way, he found the bad news to be encouraging—now, at last, things were starting to move, and they were configuring themselves into a familiar pattern. "It means we're moving into the next stage."

"Next stage of what?"

"Psy-war," he said. "Psy-war and disinformation. You almost have to admire these people; they're real pros. We'll start having riots next."

"Not in Denver," Captain Delrio said firmly. "Not on *my* watch."

"Then we'd better get the case solved in a hurry, Captain, because the momentum on this is building fast."

"You're asking me to stick my neck way out for you, Boone." Delrio held up her hand, with thumb and forefinger barely half a centimeter apart. "People a lot higher up in the food chain than I am are *this* close to wanting you taken off the case."

"Well, am I?"

"I'm stalling them. For now, at least—this could change at any moment." Delrio paused a moment. "I wasn't going to ask you last night on an open global link—what exactly did you *do* that made the North Dakota Staties so unhappy I had to abandon a perfectly good dinner party to go and calm them down?"

"Reinterviewed a couple of witnesses," Boone said. "Visited an empty field and looked at a deserted warehouse. Got pursued and shot at by unknown individuals driving an unmarked vehicle that allegedly wasn't there."

"Uh-huh," said Delrio. "Alleged by who, exactly—the state police?"

"You got it."

Captain Delrio looked at him for a moment. "Just between you and me, Boone—how deserted was that warehouse?"

"About two weeks' worth, judging from appearances."

"Find anything useful?"

"Not by the time the bad guys finished chasing us. Which I'll bet was the general idea. Somebody's covering stuff up, Captain . . . I wish I knew who, and what."

"So do I," Captain Delrio said. "You've been working on this for almost a week, harassing local government employees and traveling all over the country on my dime. You'd better get something definitive soon, and it had better be good enough to keep riots away from my city."

* * *

It was two o'clock. Time to leave for the *Museum*. Kate Boone read the latest message in her global's textmail window one more time:

Kind lady—

We are agreed. I will bring what I can of those things for which you asked. You will have to make your own arrangements for transporting them elsewhere.

Augur.

She'd taken heed of the last sentence especially, and was carrying a leather shoulder bag with room in its zippered compartments for a handheld computer and a stack of solid media in different shapes and sizes. And if that wasn't room enough, the tailored white suit jacket she'd chosen to wear for the occasion had both outer and inner pockets as well. So long as she didn't have to pass through any X-ray machines, she could smuggle her data like a pro.

She'd left the big main compartment of her shoulder bag empty, in case she needed to take away printouts of anything. That meant she had to distribute the essential bits of its former contents among her various pockets: driver's license, electronic check register, house keys, mini-toolkit, pencils, and paper. It took a bit of work to make the sides balance so that the jacket still hung right when she was done.

The last thing she did, before locking the door and embarking upon her first venture into actual fieldwork, was to go out to her rose garden and snip one of the early crimson buds. She affixed the flower to her jacket with a long hatpin—why do people still call them hatpins? she wondered; nobody wears hats like that any more—squared her shoulders, and started on her way.

She'd spent considerable time thinking about where to meet with her unknown correspondent, the mysterious Augur, before settling on the Museum of Natural History as the best bet. The museum provided plenty of visual distraction, in the form of exhibits and people looking at exhibits; one more person come to visit the Mayan frescos or the butterfly collection wasn't likely to be noticed. The museum also had lots of different ways in and out, all noted in pink highlighter on Kate's printout of the floor plan, and lots of unobtrusive security.

She hoped that the jacket and the rose were enough to identify her to Augur, or that he had in fact been able to locate one of her old ID photos. She certainly had no idea how she'd go about recognizing him.

When she reached the museum, she walked slowly from the IMAX theater toward the planetarium, pretending as she did so that she had a genuine interest in the displays meant to teach school children about "Your Weight on Mars" and "How Hot Is the Sun." According to the brochure she'd picked up when she entered the museum, the planetarium's sky show this month dealt with the ancient Greeks and the constellations. There wasn't much of a line for the next showing; the coming of the Companions, Kate thought, had made that sort of thing moot.

There weren't gods and heroes in the sky anymore, there were tall blue creatures that spoke strange whispering words and promised peace and plenty for all.

She was inspecting the display on cometary orbits and killer asteroids for the third time when a muscular young man wearing a Caribbean-cut sleeveless shirt and short trousers stepped up beside her.

"Shrew?" the man said.

She turned for a better view. Considered objectively, she thought, it was a view worth turning for. His facial features were a striking mix of black and Oriental, accentuated by a closely trimmed mustache and goatee. His head was entirely shaven, except for a tight braid at the back of his skull.

His glasses had red-tinted lenses that glinted strangely in the subdued museum light: interface lenses, able to pick up and project a heads-up display, and not an affectation so much as wearable advertising for an information professional with at least one foot dipped into murky waters. Kate understood their message—*Not everything you see here is going to be legal*—as much as she knew that her suburban garden-club matron appearance conveyed a message of its own: *If you don't want to deal with the straight and narrow, go somewhere else.*

It was nice, she thought, to know from the beginning where everyone stood. Now they could start the dance. She met the man's eyes directly.

"Should I know you?"

"You asked to see me," he said. He quoted the first five digits of her security code. "Now do you know my name?"

She narrowed her eyes. "I might. It wouldn't be Seer, or Haruspex, or something like that, would it?"

"Close, but no cigar. And it isn't Rumpelstiltskin, either."

"Augur."

"Once is enough," he cautioned her. "Anyone could be listening, and someone probably is."

"Welcome to Paranoid World."

"I prefer to think of it as being adequately cautious."

"Have it your way," she said. They were strolling now as they talked, tending away from the planetarium and toward the rock and mineral displays. "You wanted a meeting, and now you've got one. How about telling me more about this mutual friend you say we've got?"

"Ah, yes, your husband. The estimable Captain Boone. I'm afraid that certain people have fed him misleading information in the hopes of making me seem like a criminal. I'd appreciate it if you could tell him that I'm not guilty of those deeds which are being attached to my name."

"He has an office and a published global number. You can tell him that yourself."

"The unfortunate thing," Augur said, "is that I *am* a criminal. For certain values of 'crime.' My talking with your husband directly would put both of us in an unhappy position."

"So you want me to play go-between," she said. "These 'certain people' of yours—name names, or I'm out of here."

Augur shook his head. "The names would mean little to you, or to him. Let me tell you what they're doing. They have a lab set up, where they are producing false corpses, and where they are manufacturing evidence that the Taelons mean us harm, that they aren't our friends."

"Why should you care what people say about the Taelons?"

"I don't," he said frankly. "But being arrested and falsely imprisoned for taking part in Taelon atrocities would adversely affect my ability to do business. And I don't want that."

"I want the names," she said again. "Without those, your story is nothing more than unsubstantiated rumor. Names, on the other hand, can be checked and verified."

"You drive a hard bargain, kind lady. The names, then: An Army colonel named Menendez is a tool in the hands of certain people who wish to destabilize the United States. These people—call them the destabilizers—believe that the Taelons don't care who's actually running the various countries here on Earth so long as everything down here stays calm and nonviolent. So the destabilizers plan to carry out a coup d'etat, after which the Taelons will step in to prevent the overthrow of the new regime by the old loyal forces, and then the rest will be—"

Kate's vision blacked out. She pulled in her breath

to scream, and sucked cloth into her mouth instead. At the same moment, she felt a heavy blow land in her stomach. She doubled over in pain. A moment later, she felt the sting of an injection in her arm, and consciousness spiraled down to a pinpoint of identity and went dark.

—text of message sent by [NAME DELETED BY ARCHIVE SECURITY], Seattle, Washington, to Captain Will Boone, Denver Police Department; flagged "urgent."

Captain Boone:

I write to you at the request of a former associate from the wartime years. Please reply from your home terminal with a blank message to this mail-drop, subject line Awaiting Developments.

Sincerely,
[NAME DELETED]
[SIGNATURE BLOCK APPENDED]

EIGHTEEN

After his conference with Captain Delrio, the remainder of Boone's working day passed uneventfully—a good thing, considering his present exhausted state. He spent the time at his desk, catching up on the routine paperwork that had accumulated during this latest road trip; for a couple of hours in midafternoon, he caught up with some of his lost sleep as well, leaning back in his swivel chair and dozing where he sat. He even dreamed, fitfully, of sitting down for dinner, and tasting pot roast and gravy that turned to a cheap greaseburger as he chewed.

Too many meals on the road this week, he decided after he had shaken himself awake again. He must be getting old; back in his Army days, he could live off of roots, berries, and field rations for a month or longer before he started dreaming about Kate's home cooking.

He slogged through the rest of the day, and left work as early as he thought he could get away with, which wasn't much. Captain Delrio was a firm believer in having the captains and lieutenants set a good example for the rest of the police officers in the department. It was past five in the afternoon before he was able to leave his desk and drive home to the Denver suburb where he and Kate had settled two years before.

Kate's car wasn't in the garage when he got there, but that wasn't unusual—she had freelance work of her own to take care of, after all, not to mention the household errands he'd been letting slide for the past week—and he wasn't surprised, at first, to find the house deserted. The kitchen was cold, though, and empty, with nothing roasting in the oven or simmering on the range, and no little bowls of diced meat and chopped vegetables lined up to await their final rendezvous with a wok.

There was a note on the refrigerator door, scribbled on a torn-off piece of green and white computer paper and held in place with a magnet shaped like a cow:

Will—went out to meet the person you talked about. If I'm not back by two P.M., start the search at the Museum of Natural History, near rocks and gems. —Kate

Two P.M. had come and gone three hours ago. Feeling suddenly cold, Boone punched Kate's code into his global.

Nobody answered. No still pic of her features, no real-time video feed, no audio. Only the please-leave-a-message screen, which was still the same flat blue as it had been when Kate's global came home from the electronics shop for the first time.

That was wrong. Kate had customized the message screen almost before she did anything else with her new electronic toy. With a sense of increasing desperation, he used his global to check his E-mail queue. Nothing there from Kate, either. Only a message from a Seattle corporate address that he almost trashed in spite of its "urgent" flag.

But with Kate gone missing, anything anomalous could be important. He opened the message.

His first thought was, Damn. I don't have time for these games right now.

Then he thought again. Kate had gone to meet with "the person he'd talked about," which could only mean Augur. She hadn't come back, and her global wasn't answering properly. And now somebody was trying to get in touch. That was bad.

One more thing to check. He called the police bullpen and asked the duty sergeant if there'd been any untoward occurrences reported today at the Natural History Museum.

"Sorry, sir," the sergeant said. "I don't see anything in the log. What kind of thing were you looking for?"

"Anything out of the usual."

"Can't help you there, Captain," said the sergeant. "We haven't had any calls to that address today."

"Right," Boone said. "Thanks."

For a moment Boone wondered if he'd really talked with the duty sergeant—or had the officer been some kind of a fake, the product of voice emulation and digital imagery, like that report from Montana?

No matter, and no way to tell. Will walked across

the kitchen and leaned against the wall, his shoulders sagging. Kate wasn't supposed to get involved in this kind of thing. He'd labored hard, all the time he was in the Army, to keep his life with her separate from the dirt and backstabbing of his work for Special Ops; it wasn't fair that she should get pulled into it now that he was a civilian.

Boone thought for a moment longer, then reached a decision. He pulled out his wallet and found the card that Eyeglasses had given him after their secret meeting near D.C. The call code was on the back. He punched the code into his global, waited a moment while the signal went out, and, as soon as the connection was made, immediately broke it.

That was step one. Now for step two. Boone went from the kitchen to the den. There he flipped the desk computer out of sleep mode, opened his mail agent, and sent a blank message headed "Awaiting Developments" to the Seattle address,

Then he went back into the kitchen and made himself a sandwich—cold smoked turkey and whole-wheat pita bread, the sort of things Kate bought for herself when he wasn't in town to cook for—and ate it standing up at the counter. He was enough of an old campaigner to know that he ought to grab some food while he still could. There was no telling when the next chance might be.

He was finishing the last bite of the sandwich when his global chimed. He flipped the device open.

"You called us," a voice said. The screen where the speaker's face should have been was blank. "We'll bring you in. In exactly five minutes, walk down to the foot of your front walk. There'll be a car."

"See you," Will said, and slid the global shut again. He checked his watch and walked back to the den. His mail agent had closed down, but his notepad was open. The text window should have been empty—he hadn't touched the notepad in days—but it wasn't.

The same people who are framing me got Shrew. We need to talk. Augur.

"'Shrew?'" Will said aloud. Then he remembered. "Kate."

Talk where? he typed into the notepad program. Omerta was right about how good Augur was, he reflected. The guy had climbed into his computer system somehow, and was reading text from and putting text to a program that wasn't supposed to let you do that from anywhere but the chair in front of the screen. He'd have to ask Kate how the trick was done, if he didn't screw up the next few hours of her life so badly that he never got the chance.

Someplace safe, came the reply a moment later. There was a brief pause, and then more letters appeared on the screen, quickly this time, as if the person at the other end was typing in great haste. **Changing location now. I'll be in touch.**

Then one final line:

Don't go with the people who are coming for you.

* * *

Kate woke up in a dark room.

She came back to consciousness slowly, which after

a few minutes—once she was able to think clearly again, without her mental processes blurred and muffled by the aftereffects of whatever drug had taken her under—she decided was a good thing. By the time she was fully awake, she knew that she was lying on a bed or cot of some sort (narrow enough that as she lay there, she felt one outflung arm dangling off the edge and her opposite foot hard up against some vertical surface), and that she was neither blindfolded nor bound.

It was possible, she supposed, that she had somehow lost her sight during the interval she had been unconscious, but she didn't think it was likely. She pressed her fingers against her eyelids and saw fireworks. The optic nerves were intact. Therefore, it would do her no good to panic.

She told herself this several times.

Once she was able to think about her situation without hyperventilating, she sat up—carefully, since she had no way to tell how stable the surface beneath her was, or how much overhead she had to work with—and started taking inventory, by touch, of her current possessions. Her leather shoulder bag was gone, of course. Maybe it was in the same room with her, but she didn't think that was a good bet. Stripped of identifying items and tossed into a trash bin was a better one.

Her shoes were gone; either they'd slipped off her feet during transport, or somebody had taken them away for the purpose of leaving her barefoot. They'd left her with her jacket, though—maybe to keep away the cold? The air here was chilly, and smelled of dust.

Where *was* here, anyway?

She told herself again not to panic.

Chilly, and smelled of dust. But she hadn't been left to lie on the floor, and she hadn't been tied up, and she still had her jacket. Her captors didn't want her damaged, apparently; maybe they didn't want her uncomfortable if they could help it. A hopeful sign. If they needed her in good shape, maybe it meant that she was scheduled to be released eventually.

What purpose, then, was served by her presence here?

She'd been talking with Augur when she was caught. Talking about Will. Had Augur betrayed her, or had they both fallen into the trap? She swallowed; her throat was dry, and she didn't want her first words in this place to come out in an undignified croak.

"If you can hear me, Augur, say so."

Nobody answered. The quality of the reverberation made her think that the room she occupied was fairly small. Another data point.

"If you sold me out, Augur, I've got friends who can track down your identities and turn them into shredded packing paper. And that's a promise."

She'd have to save that for later, though, if she ever got the chance. Meanwhile—Will. He had enemies, Augur had implied, possibly truthfully and possibly not. Enemies, she wondered, or awkward friends? It didn't matter; either way she was in a world of trouble.

She put a foot over the edge of the cot opposite the

wall, and felt floor beneath, cold, smooth. Maybe linoleum. She stood, with her right hand brushing the wall, and willed her feet to hold her. After a moment of swaying, she was steady. Then, hand still trailing, she paced out the room. She passed four corners before she returned to the cot, finding it by barking her shins against it. She had passed one doorway, two corners from where she started. It had a knob, but the knob didn't turn. The hinges were on the other side.

She would not panic. She would definitely not panic. She would go through her jacket pockets one at a time, by touch, and find out what she had in the line of resources.

A wrapped cough drop, the forgotten relic of last winter's final cold. No good for anything, except maybe to suck on if she got hungry.

Her electronic check register. No good in the dark, even if Will *had* given it to her last year for a birthday present. She gave a wavery laugh, remembering. He'd gotten the shop to throw in every single custom add-on in the catalog, from the pronouncing dictionary to the interactive on-line wine advisor, and he still looked a bit sad, sometimes, that all she used it for was to update her main accounting program once a week.

Didn't matter; still no damned good in the dark.

On to the next.

The hard-shell plastic case of her mini-toolkit. Not much help in the dark either, and she didn't know why they'd left it and taken her global. Maybe they'd thought that the case held cosmetics, or some other bit of feminine paraphernalia—men embarrassed so easily, sometimes. Or maybe they'd taken a quick glance inside, seen the needle and thread and the folding scissors, and not bothered to look any further.

Next.

Keychain. House keys, car keys, the key to her old briefcase, a padlock key for she-didn't-remember-what, a police whistle—how long has *that* been on there? she wondered, and couldn't remember—and a small plastic disk with an inset button.

"Damn," she said aloud. "I am stupid. Or full of stupid-making drugs. I should have remembered this."

She pressed the button, and had barely enough time for a fleeting thought—if the battery is dead I'm going to feel *so* stupid—before the light came on.

A pale and narrow beam of light, since the tiny flashlight had only been designed to find a keyhole in the dark, and she hadn't replaced its battery since she'd bought it four or five changes of residence ago, but a light. Enough to reveal the dimensions of her cell—an ordinary room, really, reminiscent of some of the barracks she'd seen during Will's army career.

With a light switch on the far wall, and a lock—a cipher lock—on the door.

For the first time since she'd regained consciousness, Kate began to smile.

—text of message sent by Kate Boone to [NAME DELETED BY ARCHIVE SECURITY], Gaithersburg, Maryland.

I'm looking at some very interesting files. Your name turns up in an awful lot of them. I can't say that ! think highly of your friends.

Did you sell me out on purpose, or was it just an accident?

—Shrew

NINETEEN

The line of text—**Don't go with the people who are coming for you**—glowed for a moment longer on the computer screen before it winked out.

Boone looked at his watch. Two minutes left. He had to make up his mind, and do it quickly: Should he trust the people he'd spoken with in Washington, men he'd worked and fought beside, and whoever they were sending around locally, or should he believe the warning from a known criminal?

He checked his weapon. He opened his desk drawer, fished around, and dropped a second magazine into his coat pocket. One minute left. Time to choose.

The answer was obvious: "I'm a cop. I chase criminals."

He took a step backward and raised his pistol, firing twice in rapid succession into the central processing unit and the hard drive of his desktop computer. A flash of blue light and thin streamers of acrid white smoke curled out of the unit's media slots.

There, Boone thought. No one will be getting any data out of that box for a while.

Thirty seconds left.

He turned and headed for the rear of the house. By the time he'd reached the kitchen and eased open the door to the back steps, heavy knocks were already sounding at the front.

The backyard had a tall privacy fence surrounding it, and no gate—there was nothing on the other side but a neighboring yard. On the other hand, Kate's compost bin was right up against the boards of the fence. Boone used the bin as a stepping-stone to climb up and over. Once he was in the next yard he walked briskly around that house to the street, and continued walking for several minutes, until he had left his old neighborhood behind.

His global chimed. Still walking, he pulled it from his pocket and slid it open. A blank screen appeared, with pale letters on it; somebody was sending through the text-only channels. Probably bounced all over the world to lose the trail on the way.

Augur here. Imperative we meet and talk.

"No argument from me on that," Boone said. "Where?"

My place this time.

"You don't keep a high profile. I'll need directions."

Coming your way.

The letters on the screen vanished. A moment later, an image appeared: a interactive city map showing two bright red dots. One dot marked the suburb where Boone and Kate had their house. The other was on the far side of town, in what could most charitably be described as a rough industrial neighborhood. An inset map at the bottom left of the screen displayed a smaller area extending a few blocks in each direction from the street corner on which Boone stood. A line of blinking red dots extended two blocks north from that center point, then turned one block left.

"You realize that sending in the clear like this is risky," Boone said. "Eavesdroppers could—"

No time for you to memorize directions, SpecOps man. The line of text appeared for an instant at the bottom of the smaller map, then blinked out and was replaced by another. **Better start walking.**

Global in hand, Boone complied. After he had walked for the two blocks and made the turn, he pressed the screen. The inset map shifted slightly. The dotted line now extended for three more blocks in the new direction before taking the right-hand fork at a Y junction. Boone continued on, following the new directions, and let the map lead him away from the quiet suburban streets toward wider and busier thoroughfares.

His global chimed again. A new line of text had appeared underneath the map.

You're going too slow. Move faster.

"I'm proceeding on foot at the moment. This is as fast as it gets."

Get some transportation.

"Easy for you to say. Type. Whatever."

This spot's not good for much longer before I have to move again. Blink; then a new line of text: **Can you get here inside two hours?**

"Not without running," he said, after contemplating the map. "And running is a bad idea. Conspicuous."

Any better ideas?

"Give me a minute." Boone tapped in a new code on his global. The map screens shrank to a couple of pyramids down in one corner of the display, and Lieutenant Bob Morovsky's features appeared in the main viewer.

"Listen, Bob," Boone said. "I need you to get an unmarked car as soon as possible—fifteen minutes ago would be about right—and meet me with it at the corner of Poplar and Benton."

"Sure thing. Do I get an explanation once I'm there?"

"Maybe later," Boone said. "I'm short on time at the moment."

"The things I do for my friends," Morovsky said. "See you soon."

His image vanished from the global's screen and the maps came back. **Are you still hanging around in the same spot?** demanded the text at the bottom of the smaller map. **You need to keep moving.**

"Don't worry. I'm working on it."

He punched in another code before Augur could type a reply. This time, the image that replaced the maps was the rocklike face of Sergeant Omerta.

"Sergeant," Boone said. "I need a backdoor-protocol lock-and-trace on two globals, as fast as you can arrange it. Grid-posit of their physical locations."

To Omerta's credit, he didn't waste time asking for explanations. "Which two?"

"My wife's, for one. Name's Kate Boone, the address is the same as mine and you've got that address on file. I'm worried that she may be in trouble."

Which was not strictly the truth, he reflected. He *knew* that Kate was in trouble. It was all the other details that he was short on.

"Working that one," said Omerta after a moment. "We'll pass the word along as soon as we get a hit."

"Thanks."

"What about the second search? Who do you want?"

"Me. I want you to run the lock-and-trace location on my global, too."

This time Omerta did look curious. "What for?"

"I'll tell you later," Boone promised. "Just do it, okay?—and keep me posted."

"Safe to call on this channel?"

"Nothing's safe. Talk to you later. I think I have the guy we're both interested in."

"Now I'm interested too. I'll be in touch."

Boone shut that window and opened up the connection back to Augur. The map was blinking.

Transportation?

"I'm working on it," he said to the open channel.

Other people are working on you, the line of text came back. **I can block them, but they won't stay blocked for long. Shorter if they're clever.**

"Tell me what happened today."

When we meet.

He didn't reply. The line of text faded from the map screen, and no more comments from Augur appeared during the time it took for Morovsky to arrive with the unmarked car. The wait was long enough to make Boone uneasy—the older cop was known to be working with him on the current case, and could have run into trouble on that account—but at last a green sedan with Morovsky at the wheel rounded the corner and pulled up to the curb.

Boone opened the door and slid into the front passenger seat. "High time you got here."

"Wouldn't have wanted to break any traffic laws," Morovsky said. "Where to now?"

"Warehouse district. I'll take it from there on my own."

His global blinked at him. **If you're with someone,** the line of text on the screen said, **remember, if I see anyone besides you, then you won't see me.**

"Okay," Morovsky said.

"Okay," Boone echoed, but he wasn't talking to his partner. He closed the global and tucked it back inside his jacket.

They drove in silence for some time. After a while, Morovsky said, "Mind telling me what this is all about?"

"Kate's gone missing," Boone said. "I have a note from her."

"Is this a police matter? Or can I help?"

"I don't think so," Boone said. He looked out the window at the grimy industrial streets that surrounded them, now that they were away from both the nice suburbs and the central city. "This is about as close as you need to get . . . that corner right up there would be fine, in fact. Slow down to about five miles per hour as soon as you make the turn."

"Whatever you want," Morovsky said. "But good cops don't hold out on their partners, and they don't go anywhere without backup."

"Who ever told you I was a good cop?" Boone asked. His hand was already on the door handle.

As soon Morovsky turned the corner, Boone opened the door and rolled out. He fetched up beside a wall, unhurt, and scuttled backward into concealment beside a trash bin, then crouched in the shadows as Morovsky accelerated again and pulled away. He wasn't surprised to see another car, a large black van this time, come around the corner a moment later and continue along the same track that Morovsky had taken. He was relieved, though, when it kept on going.

He took the global from his pocket and slid it open. In spite of the drop-and-roll, the device was still intact and functioning. The map switched to show a particular warehouse, not far from the trash bin where he currently huddled.

Boone stood, straightened his clothes, dusted himself, and started hiking. He also unsnapped the thumb latch on his holster. Maybe he wouldn't go in to this meeting with weapon in hand, but he didn't intend to waste time fumbling if his combat reflexes told him that things were going horribly wrong.

The warehouse indicated on the map was right ahead. Boone figured that he was under surveillance already, so he didn't do any dodging around.

If Augur wants me, he can have me, he thought.

He was wearing his standard police lightweight body armor—he hadn't had a chance to take it off, between arriving home and starting out again—not that wearing the armor gave him any comfort. Anyone tracking him would know that he was a cop and likely to be wearing a vest, and their sniper would already have a head shot lined up. All that kept him going was the knowledge that if Augur truly had wanted him dead, the man wouldn't have needed to go to all this trouble just in order to kill him.

The warehouse had a sliding door on a loading dock with a regular man-sized door beside it. Boone walked up to the door and turned the knob. The door opened.

The screen on the global said **Welcome**.

—text of message from Kate Boone to [NAME DELETED BY ARCHIVE SECURITY], Gaithersburg, Maryland

Never mind how I got onto this account.

You said:

>Nobody was supposed to hurt you

What did you =think= they were going to do—send me champagne and a box of chocolates?

Passing along private messages to third parties is the act of a low form of sentient life, and you did it anyway. Just tell me one thing: Did you do all those image manipulation and data-fakery jobs out of a sense of principle, or was it just another contract gig?

—Shrew

TWENTY

Boone walked through the door. The far side of the big enclosed space towered with boxes and crates stuffed with the detritus of the electronic life. Ancient computer cases filled a wire cage, along with circuit boards, spools of wire, and cartons with red stamps reading SILICON CIRCUITS: DO NOT IRRADIATE. Skylights overhead illuminated the warehouse, casting shadows from chainfalls and overhead cranes, a mix of nineteenth-, twentieth-, and twenty-first-century tech all in one location.

The room was spookily silent. Boone looked down at his global, but whoever had been calling him had broken the connection. Boone closed the global, put it in his pocket, and pulled his weapon. Then he started walking between the cliffs of technological junk.

Halfway toward the back, on the left-hand side, he came to an arrow drawn with spray paint, still wet, on a piece of cardboard that otherwise sported an IBM logo and a series of product numbers.

The arrow pointed him toward a door set into the wall. Again, the door was unlocked. Boone opened it, and stepped into a small chamber beyond with a second door a few feet from the first. The outer door closed.

"Please drop your gun into the box," an amplified voice said from overhead.

"Okay," Boone replied. The box was a velvet-lined container bolted to the left-hand wall.

"Now the gun from your ankle," the voice said.

"Okay," Boone replied again, as he complied. He'd come this far, he'd see how the game played out.

"Are you carrying anything else that could hurt me?" the voice asked.

"Just a dangerous attitude," Boone said. "And it isn't getting any better."

"Voice stress analysis says you're telling the truth," the voice said. "Welcome to my home."

The inner door opened, and Boone stepped through. The inner room was full of monitor displays and blinking lights and large pieces of unidentifiable hardware. Or at least hardware that Boone couldn't identify—Kate would know what they were, he thought; and then, Kate isn't here. That's the whole problem.

Instead, he had the owner, or at any rate the occupant, of this technological magpie's nest: a young black man with a partially shaven head and gaudy wire-rimmed spectacles. Augur reminded Boone of the information specialists he'd known during his time in Special Operations, strange solitary men and women more accustomed to interfacing with their own computer terminals than with ordinary people.

"Okay," Boone said. "I'm here. You wanted to talk with me. Let's talk."

"First I have something to show you."

Augur turned back to his control panel, a bank of monitor screens and multiple keyboards that looked like it could have been part of the original U.S. space program. For all Boone knew, it had been. Augur tapped in a code sequence and brought up an image on one of the screens.

"I went out looking for information," he said, "and I found this. Low-light/IR TV. Live feed from a security cam to a control room."

The picture showed a slim, fair-haired woman in a summer-weight business suit, lying on an army cot with her arms hugging her chest. Her feet were bare. Boone took an involuntary step closer as the woman in the picture shifted, turning on her side and drawing up her knees as far as she could on the narrow cot.

"That's my wife," Boone said. "That's Kate."

"Yes."

Boone deliberately turned away from the image on the monitor. Watching any more of it would be dangerous; the fear and anger would break out of the mental compartment where he had put them away. He had to stay calm, if he was going to be of any help to Kate at all.

"Where is she?"

"I've got a location. Will you help me?"

"That depends." Boone took another step closer to Augur, deliberately crowding into the shorter man's personal space and forcing him backward. "Do you have anything to do with Kate being held in there? And is *this*—" he gestured at the instrument-filled space around them "—the control room that you mentioned, that the feed from the security video goes to?"

"You wound me," Augur said. Boone gave him points, reluctantly, for maintaining his aplomb under stress. "I'm indirectly responsible for her being there, yes. If she'd stayed home tending her roses rather than trying to meet with me she might be cooking your dinner right now. But no, I didn't order your wife's present incarceration, nor am I responsible for keeping her there."

"Then who is?"

"A group of individuals calling themselves the Gamma Organization. They have certain romantic ideas about resisting the Companions."

"And you?"

"I have my own romantic ideas, but they mostly concern sprawling on a golden throne while nubile young ladies in transparent harem pants feed me hothouse grapes." Augur looked Boone up and down. "I expect that you have a few romantic ideas yourself, all about truth, beauty, and the rule of law."

Boone gave a brief laugh. "The Boy Scout law, if you must know."

"You're an altruistic man, Captain Boone."

"And you're a self-interested one?"

"Exactly. And my plans—golden throne and all—

will be spoiled if Earth gets laid waste from high orbit. My plans will also be ruined if humanity becomes nothing more than a supine and subjugated people. This makes me both friend and enemy to either side—and so I have perfect freedom."

"Including the freedom to swindle old ladies?"

"I have never provided a business opportunity to anyone who didn't truly want it."

Me included, Boone thought. Aloud, he added, "You said that you'd tell me what happened today with Kate. First, tell me why you were meeting with my wife at all."

"Don't be jealous," Augur said. "Our conversation was all about you."

"Anybody ever told you that you have a sick sense of humor?"

Augur sketched a half-bow. "It's a gift."

"I'll bet it is. Why did you set up that meeting, Augur?"

The other man didn't answer directly. "Certain members of the Gamma Organization apparently believed that since I have been known to cooperate—they would say, to collaborate—with the Taelons from time to time, I would make an acceptable scapegoat for their own misdeeds."

"They were framing you."

"In essence, yes."

"For what?" Boone asked; then answered his own question. "Those mutilation murders—the 'experiments'—they're being faked by this Gamma Organization, in order to stir up public sentiment against the Taelons. And you chanced upon their nefarious activities purely by accident, I suppose."

"In the course of my day-to-day business," Augur agreed. "And I was instantly filled with the desire to do my duty as a citizen by informing the police officer in charge of the case. Unfortunately, there were a few stumbling blocks in the way."

"Those 'business opportunities' of yours."

"Among other things. So I attempted to make contact with you through a more informal channel."

Boone's gaze went back to Kate's image on the security monitor. She was asleep, but moving restlessly on the cot—had they hurt her? Was she drugged?

"There are any number of ways you could have contacted me," he said. "Why use my wife?"

"Connections," Augur said. "We have old friends and business associates in common, the Shrew and I. She came very well vouched for, I can assure you."

"All those connections didn't keep her from getting snatched while you were with her."

"No," Augur admitted. "But—given that the kidnappers seized her and left me behind—there's a distinct possibility that she was taken not because she'd just spoken with me, but in order that she might later speak with you."

Boone forced himself to look away from the image on the monitor. "I wish you hadn't said that."

"It's the curse of an inventive mind. Have you checked your global lately, Captain Boone?"

"No . . . . damn. I wish you hadn't said that, either." Cursing under his breath, Boone pulled the device out of his coat pocket and slid it open. The message waiting screen display came up, and a moment later a voice, Kate's voice:

"Go back to the office, Will, if you aren't there right now. Go back to the office and let the world know that it was the Taelons who've been killing animals and people for experiments all along. I'm all right now, Will, and I think they'll let me go real soon now if you just do what you ought to do."

There was a long, silent moment; then Boone slid his global back shut so hard it almost slammed. "Damn."

"You see?" said Augur. "But if it's any consolation—"

"No. It isn't."

"—then my guess is that her voice was faked. Given that the Gamma Organization has the technical ability to create false messages, why should they risk letting her make a genuine communication?"

"You may have a point."

"I generally do. Are you planning to follow their strongly worded suggestion?"

"No," Boone said. "First I'm going to break Kate out of that cell. Then I'm going to smash the Gamma Organization into bits the size of pencil erasers. You said you had a location for her?"

"Right. She's being held, near as I can pin down the signal, at the site of an old Nike missile complex outside the city. There's a whole bunch of abandoned government buildings, mostly underground." Augur laughed. "Funny what things people used to worry about."

"I'm going out there."

"I thought you would be," Augur said. "There's a car around the side. Keys are in it. It's clean."

Yeah, right, Boone thought. Not counting whatever bugs and tracking devices you've got installed.

Aloud, he said, "I'll need my handguns."

"No problem. Pick 'em up on your way out. You'll have to leave your global behind with me, though—you don't want to allow the Gamma Organization to contact you directly. There's another global waiting for you in the car. It's been twinned to your original: Anyone punching in your code will get you; anyone you call will see the message as coming from you. The only difference is that everything's bouncing through here."

"Allowing you to hear everything I say."

Augur smiled at Boone serenely. "Why should tonight be different from any other night? Move on out, SpecOps man—daylight's burning."

The drive out to the missile base took over two hours, even with Boone pushing the upper margin of the speed limit all the way. He left the car about a mile down the road from where the base's outer perimeter touched the highway, and walked back.

"I'm here," he said to Augur over his global. "I should be inside the fence in just a couple of minutes."

Good. Augur had switched back to text mode—less traceable, Boone supposed. **Kate's still in the cell. Once you're inside, I can guide you around the human guards.**

"I'll hold you to that," Boone said. "And Augur—?"

Yes?

"Don't even think about selling me out. Or you *will* regret it."

—message from Kate Boone to [NAME DELETED BY ARCHIVE SECURITY], Gaithersburg, Maryland

No, I'm not going to tell you where I'm posting from.

Whose side are you on here? Better make up your mind, and do it fast.

—Shrew

TWENTY-ONE

The corridor was both long and dark, with pipes and ductwork running along the top. Doors opened off of it at random intervals along either sides. The floor was linoleum, in a green and black checkerboard pattern that had worn to dullness over the years since the base had been closed.

Will Boone hadn't encountered anyone since he'd climbed over the chain-link fence at the base perimeter and made his way to the entrance of the underground complex where—if Augur could be trusted—Kate was held prisoner. Boone was beginning to suspect that the Gamma Organization was a relatively small group, perhaps one richer in highly-placed connections than in foot soldiers on the ground.

Which would explain why they're trying to stir up anti-Taelon sentiment in the general public, Boone thought. *They're having a membership drive.*

Well, good for them. By the time I'm done, they'll wish they'd bought a mailing list and sent out postcards.

Thanks, in fact, to Augur, Boone didn't lack for

resources—this clearly wasn't the first time that the man had run mapping and communications for a covert assault. The vehicle he'd supplied for Boone had come equipped with more than keys and fuel and a clean global. A cardboard box on the passenger-side seat had turned out to contain an assortment of electronic penetration and surveillance gear.

Boone now wore low-light night vision goggles around his head, and a throat mike carried his barely vocalized words to the global for transmission. His ears were clear, so that he could detect the slightest sound around him. Going into the underground complex had required him to choose between his handgun and his flashlight, and he'd chosen his handgun. The Glock was in his right hand; his left hand held his global, its screen extended.

The screen of the global showed the room where Kate was imprisoned. She lay as he had seen her before at Augur's warehouse, in restless sleep on the bare mattress of an army cot. The view was in the green-tones of an infrared camera.

"Where to now?" Boone whispered, the words too soft to be heard more than an inch beyond his nose. "I'm at the T intersection. The door across from me reads '101.'"

Turn left, came the printed reply, scrolling along the bottom of the global's screen. **You still have to get down one level.**

Boone swung wide at the corner—"slicing the pie," as the police termed the move—so that any lurkers on the other side would come under observation and be covered by his weapon before they could react. But this corridor, like the ones before it, stretched out on ahead, empty except for the echoes and the dust of years.

"I'm already at least two levels underground," Boone whispered. "Where am I?"

"**You're in a maze of twisty little passages, all alike**, Augur's scrolling text reply read a moment later. **Go forward two hundred meters, then look for a branch or side corridor to your right.**

"You'd better be right, Augur," Boone said. "There's a lot riding on this."

I'm tapped right into their database, and I'm pulling the raw feed from their spycams.

"And I'm the one tiptoing around in the dark," Boone whispered back. "Do they have any human guards?"

None listed, Augur replied. **Maybe they have trouble hiring reliable help.**

Boone continued in silence. Kate was still in the room that Augur had identified, and still apparently unhurt. She'd been asleep like that for a long time, though. He began to entertain thoughts about head injuries and drug reactions, and had to force himself to stop.

He arrived at the crossing corridor. "Where to now?"

Go right, and follow the right side of the corridor. Count three doorways, then stop.

Boone turned right. In the night vision goggles, shapes appeared as crude blocks of lighter and darker shades of gray. There were no shadows to give depth, only relative size to indicate how far away a thing was. The wall was a series of gray tiles, with gray rectangles where doors were cut in them.

"I'm there."

The door beside you should open onto a stairway, leading down. Take it.

"Okay."

Boone stood beside the stairway door and pressed the lever. Then he flattened himself against the wall to one side of the door, and swung it open with his extended arm. Only when this action was rewarded by no more than an open door did he step through, quickly, on a diagonal. It was a stairway, all right, and he was on the landing. Down he went, stepping carefully, weapon in front of him, pointing the way.

Down a flight, through another door, left, then right, then, at last, he stood before the door which—Augur assured him—contained Kate. No guards, still; but this door, unlike most of the others he'd seen so far, had been retrofitted with a cipher lock.

"You see that?" he whispered over the throat mike.

Standard piece of off-the-rack hardware. Not to worry.

"My wife is on the other side of that door, Augur. If you can't crack the lock, I'm going to use the crude analog method and try shooting my way in."

Bad idea. Very bad idea. Be patient, SpecOps man, and I'll feed you the numbers.

"I'm waiting."

Try 314159.

Boone tucked the global into his pocket, freeing his left hand to manipulate the keypad on the cipher lock. He entered the numbers one at a time, then pushed the door open and stepped in.

The inside of the room was dark, even through night-vision goggles. But there was the cot, there was the bare mattress, and . . . no Kate.

Boone swung around in a full circle, his weapon in a two-handed combat grip. No one in sight.

"Damn." He pulled out his global and slid it open. The picture showed Kate still lying on the bare mattress of an army cot. "Augur, you got the wrong door. She's somewhere else."

The map matches up, Boone. This is the room.

"Then why aren't I in the picture? Where's Kate?"

Perhaps an answer appeared on the screen. Boone wasn't looking. He put the global back into his pocket, pulled the night vision goggles up onto his forehead to uncover his eyes, and took out his mini-flashlight. He squinted, and flicked the flashlight on.

The room opened out into color, with a small spot of light. The cot was there, and with the increased light Boone could see that a square of paper lay on the bare mattress. He walked over, still straining with every nerve for a sound or a sight that would tell him what was going on.

The paper had writing on it. Boone squatted to look at the scrap of paper without touching it. The writing was in pencil, in Kate's distinctive hand.

"Didn't anybody ever tell you not to put a data

wrangler into the same room with a cipher lock?" it read. The note was signed "The Shrew."

"Are you getting all this?" Boone asked. He slid open the global and pointed it at the note. When he looked at the screen again, the display still showed Kate imprisoned, and a new text running across the bottom of the screen.

Wonderful woman! I think I've fallen in love.

"Sorry, Augur. She's already taken."

Alas, alas, for those things that never can be. She's also out and moving, and she's foxed their own security systems. That's an endless loop recording of her in there. She's done it.

"So what are we going to do?"

Force the issue.

The regular lights in the room came up at full intensity, hurting Boone's eyes, and elsewhere in the station an alarm bell started to ring and an annunciator blatted out, "Security alert, security alert, intruder in the complex."

"This was your doing?" Boone demanded—not whispering any longer, but raising his voice enough for someone on the other side of the room to hear. He imagined Augur, back at the warehouse, pulling off a pair of earphones, his ears smarting to match Boone's still-watering eyes.

The global scene changed too, to show the empty cell, with its bare mattress. Boone flattened himself against the wall beside the door, where the global told him he was out of sight from the monitoring camera. Then, suddenly and unexpectedly, his global chimed.

Boone punched the button to answer the call, splitting his attention between it and the door. Lieutenant Omerta appeared on the screen.

"Captain Boone. I got the location on those globals—"

"This line is *not* secure," Boone interrupted in a low hiss. "The first one that I asked about, where is it now?"

"Old Nike base off northwest of town."

"Check. Get with Bob Morovsky and Captain Delrio, tell them that you're interested. Got me?"

"Got you."

"The second one. Answer yes or no. Do you have a posit on it?"

"Yes."

"Good. That's all I need to hear. Talk with Bob and the captain. I'll have something for everyone soon."

With that Boone closed the global. This time he set the ringer to silent before he put the device away. Then, holding his pistol, he waited, to see who might come through the door.

He didn't have to wait long before a man sidestepped through the door and took a crouch, holding a weapon on Boone. Lieutenant Omerta.

"Darned right you'll have something for everyone," Omerta said. "Put down the gun, Boone. You've gone over to the other side. I got a posit on your global, all right. It's in one of the three possible areas where Augur's located."

Boone slowly placed his pistol on the floor. "You're making a mistake," he said.

"Kick it over there, in the corner," Omerta said, nodding at the pistol. "I don't think I'm making any mistake. Let's go upstairs where you can explain it to my boss."

Boone found the trip upstairs, made in full light and by the quickest route, to be far more nerve-racking than the slow painstaking trip into the depths of the complex, possibly because he hadn't been in handcuffs on the way in. He wasn't reassured when, on the upper levels, Omerta was joined by some of the base guards whom he'd previously missed—a quartet of heavily armed individuals dressed in black uniforms with black balaclavas masking their features.

The control room where he was taken contained two more of the armed guards, a desk, and a chair, the latter occupied by his Washingtonian acquaintance with the metal-rimmed eyeglasses. There was no chair for Boone.

"You were instructed to wait for pickup," Eyeglasses said. "You didn't. Instead, you went to one of the aliens' known confederates. Why?"

"Events seemed to warrant it. I was tasked with looking for Taelon involvement in human misfortunes; so far I haven't seen any evidence of that, but I *have* seen plenty of evidence for falsified data. Is that your doing?"

Eyeglasses didn't answer him directly. "Do you plan to exonerate the Taelons in your final report? That's a poor repayment for the help you got when the Army decided it couldn't use your talents anymore."

"I don't recall you even being present at that

meeting," Boone said. "If you had been, you'd know that I agreed to keep my eyes open—not to shut them."

There was a long silence while Eyeglasses looked at Boone with cold, thoughtful eyes. Finally he spoke again, this time in a conversational, almost friendly tone.

"There was always a problem with using artificially manufactured corpses to create incidents. Lacking true identities, they left no one behind to express concern over their supposed deaths. But if the brave police officer who was investigating the Taelons becomes the next person to turn up murdered by them—then *this* time, I hope, people will sit up and take notice."

"And do what?"

"That," said Eyeglasses, "is one of the things that you won't be alive long enough to find out. Take him away."

—message from Kate Boone to [DELETED BY ARCHIVE SECURITY], Gaithersburg, Maryland

Fair enough. You give me everything you've got, and I'll make certain the delete-key fairy sprinkles her magic pixie dust over everything with your name on it.

But make it snappy. I have things to do and places to go, and people here are starting to move.

—Shrew

TWENTY-TWO

Eyeglasses sat in silence, watching, as the two black-masked guards took station behind Boone, each guard grabbing one of his upper arms, then turned and marched him out into the passageway and down to the elevator at the end of the hall. The left-hand guard pushed the DOWN button.

The elevator opened—sliding doors of plain gray-painted metal, chipped and scraped; nobody had done maintenance here for a long time, and it showed—and the guards took Boone inside. Boone thought briefly about attacking the guards and taking their weapons away, then shooting his way out, but the handcuffs were a definite obstacle. So were the cramped confines of the elevator, and the fact that he didn't know what might be waiting for him at the bottom when the doors slid open.

And somewhere on the base, there was Kate. Even if he managed to free himself from the handcuffs, he couldn't leave without finding her first.

The elevator came to the bottom of its run and the doors slid open. Ahead of him was a cavernous space—

originally some kind of storage area, Boone supposed—that had been converted into a soundstage. Floodlights illuminated a sterile-looking set, all white paint and gleaming metal, that was either the spaceship interior from Clara Grigsby's abduction or a close twin.

Cameras on dolly mounts stood ready to film the proceedings, and at a makeup table nearby another black-masked guard was helping a young woman with the back zipper of a sparkling blue jumpsuit. The Taelon head mask that she'd soon be wearing was on a wig stand beside her mirror.

"Put him in operating bay three," a male voice said—somebody outside of Boone's line of sight, speaking over a mike. "We'll go straight to the vivisection sequence and film the setup later."

In response, the guards pushed Boone around a plywood flat toward an operating table fitted with leather straps, with a tray of steel instruments beside it. Whatever else was going on, Boone had to admit that the instruments sure as hell looked alien.

"It's a real pity that we have to do this." The male speaker walked out into Boone's field of view. By now Boone wasn't surprised to find out that the man was police Lieutenant Brett Cassidy, last seen as a name on the report for a crime scene where he hadn't been present. The rot at the Denver PD, it seemed, had gone deep indeed.

"Humans shouldn't be fighting humans," Cassidy went on. "Not while there's a greater menace. But there are always casualties during wartime, and you'll have given your life in the struggle. Really, we're on the same side here."

"The Taelons will know that they didn't do this," Boone pointed out. "And they may be able to prove it."

"No one will care *what* they can prove, once your body is found." Cassidy pulled on a lab coat with a heavy rubberized apron. He spoke to a third person off somewhere in the shadows beyond the floodlights. "I think that chemically paralyzing the patient before we release his hands will be for the best."

He turned back to Boone. "We'll make it as easy for you as we can. For the greatest impact, though, your heart will still have to be beating when our Taelon friend pulls it out of your chest."

"I don't suppose you've considered using special effects for that bit?"

"Unfortunately, we can't. The heart still has to match your eventual corpse." To someone behind Boone he added, "Do you have the alien implants ready?"

The shorter of the two guards who had brought Boone down let loose his grip from Boone's right arm.

If I'm going to have a chance, Boone thought, it's going to be now. Press left, the man on my left has a broken knee. Then spin right, and hope I can find a place to run.

At least all the bullets will screw up my corpse so they can't use it.

Before he could move, he heard the rattle of beltwork as a weapon came off a man's shoulder, then the ripping sound of full-automatic fire. The sound was loud, close, deafening. The smell of powder smoke roiled about him, and the hand that gripped his left biceps was torn away as the impact of the bullets knocked the guard down to the floor. In front of him, Cassidy jerked and fell, a crimson line of bullet strikes stitching up the man's chest through the lab coat and the rubber dissection apron.

Boone didn't hesitate. He dodged left, then dashed back in the direction of the elevator as more gunfire sounded behind him. Whatever was happening, he didn't understand it. The best thing to do would be to find a safe place to figure everything out.

A shadow caught in his peripheral vision. He was being chased. The studio lights cast stark black patterns on the floor. He reached the elevator, slammed his whole body against the UP button, and flung himself in as soon as the doors slid open, hitting the back wall with a bone-jarring thud. The shadow in his peripheral vision moved with him, becoming a black-clad guard who leaped into the elevator compartment seconds before the doors slid shut.

He won't dare fire his weapon in here; Boone thought, *the bullets would rattle around like seeds in a gourd.*

Boone struggled to regain his balance preparatory to lashing out in a side-kick to the other man's kneecap. The guard threw himself back out of range and let his weapon fall clattering to the elevator floor, then reached up to pull off helmet and balaclava in a single motion.

Blonde hair, freed by the gesture, tumbled loose to

frame a suddenly familiar face. “Will? Are you all right?”

“Kate! What are you doing here?”

“I *was* just trying to get away,” she said. “But then you showed up and things got interesting. So I followed along and did what I could.”

“Where did you pick up the colorful action costume?”

“I'd say that I overpowered a guard and stripped his unconscious body, but that would be lying. I found what passes for the armory in this place and stole it. Nobody was around to stop me—there aren't really that many people here, and they're way spread out.”

“I'd noticed,” agreed Boone. “There's a handcuff key in the keeper on the back of your belt, by the way. If you wouldn't mind using it—?”

“I'll give it a try. Turn around.”

He obeyed, and felt her hands moving against his wrists as she worked the key. The metal cuffs fell away, and she said, “What do you know? It worked.”

“Of course it worked.” He turned around and kissed her briefly—no time for anything more, while they were still in enemy territory. She tasted of sweat and powder smoke, and he thought she was wonderful. “It's a standard key.”

“Nothing like off-the-rack hardware . . . what do we do now?”

“You said yourself that they don't have enough people here for adequate security. Why don't you just take me prisoner and march me up to the back gate?”

“I knew there was a reason I loved you,” Kate said.

She pushed the elevator button for the top floor. "Let's go, soldier boy."

The elevator ground slowly upward. Boone crossed his wrists behind him as if they were still cuffed. Kate put her helmet and balaclava back on and pointed her submachine gun at his back. Finally the door slid open.

"Forward, march," Kate said, pitching her voice low and making a menacing gesture with her weapon.

The subterfuge turned out to have been unnecessary. They stepped out of the elevator into an empty hallway. Boone let out a sigh of relief—too soon, as somewhere up ahead an alarm bell started to sound. Another bell echoed it distantly in the other direction.

"Sounds like somebody down in the basement finally got it together," he said. "Well, nothing to do now but keep going. Let's make this look good."

Their footsteps ringing on the linoleum tile, they continued on down to the end of the hall, where there was a door. A desk behind a glass wall stood to the right of the door. A guard dressed in black like Kate sat behind the desk.

"One to pass," Kate said.

"Access is denied during a security alert," the guard said. "You'll have to go back."

Another man stepped forward from the office opposite. This one wasn't wearing the black-fatigues-and-balaclava outfit, but a plain brown business suit. Boone recognized him at once: Sergeant Birki, late of Dog Company.

"I authorize this," Birki said. "Pass one." In Hindi he added, "I haven't forgotten that night in the Kush."

The guard pressed a button under his desk. A buzzer sounded, the door swung open, and Kate and Boone walked out into the slanting yellow sunlight of late afternoon. As soon as the door had swung shut behind them, Boone said, "Okay, follow me, run."

Then, with a rattle and a flourish, from behind crates and fences, rose more of the black-clad guards of the missile base. "We have an appointment back inside," said one of them. "Lay down your weapons."

A bullet skipped in the earth in front of the speaker. "I have a better idea," came an amplified voice from farther out. "Why don't you *all* lay down your weapons? We can figure this out downtown. On the ground, on your faces, now. Move."

"Don't argue," said Boone to Kate, pulling her down with him as men and women in the uniforms of the Denver SWAT team stepped from cover and concealment, disarming the guards. Two of them pulled Boone to his feet. Lieutenant Morovsky stepped from his own hiding place, a bullhorn in his hand.

"I came as soon as I got your message," he said to Boone. "What do you think you caught?"

"I'm not sure," Boone said. "But I'm going to find out." He gestured to the man holding Kate at rifle point on the ground. "Let that one go. She's one of the good guys."

Kate stood. She reached, slowly, inside of her shirt and pulled out a mini-disk. "This may help figure things out."

"What is it?" Morovsky asked.

"The complete texts of all electronic messages in and out of this compound over the last six months. Plus a whole bunch of other interesting stuff. I already have it decrypted."

"How?"

Kate shrugged. "I had to do something between the time I got out of the cell they were holding me in and now."

"Very nice," Morovsky said. "Let's take the disk back to headquarters along with all of these people. I'll bet Captain Delrio is dying to find out what you've got."

* * *

Some days later, Boone sat in the spare chair in Delrio's office. The senior captain was flipping through the screens of his report on her desk computer. At last she finished reading and turned to him.

"Good work, Boone. A lot of what you did doesn't apply to our jurisdiction, of course, and none of it can go public, but I think you saved the lives of a lot of people and just maybe prevented an interstellar war. Not to mention rooting out a pocket of corruption right here in our own department." She smiled briefly. "I knew that *you* were somebody's agent-in-place . . . it's a bit embarrassing to find out that there were some others I never even thought of."

"It surprised the hell out of me, too," Boone admitted. "So much for my romantic illusions."

"You'll just have to get used to being jaded and cynical like all the rest of us," said Bob Morovsky from the office doorway. He had a six-pack of colas in one hand and a pizza box balanced on the other.

"What is this," Boone asked. "A party?"

"Just an informal gathering of friends," Morovsky said. He set the pizza box down on Delrio's desk and pulled a cola out of the six-pack. He handed the can over to Boone. "You can thank me later."

"I can thank you now, too." Boone popped the top on the cola. "You never did say what alerted you to show up at the Nike base loaded for bear."

"I told you right then—you called me and told me where to come, and to come in heavy."

"Augur," Boone said.

"I expect so," said another voice, this one both familiar and unexpected, as the uniformed figure of Lieutenant-Colonel Menendez appeared in the office doorway.

"Colonel!" Boone exclaimed.

"At ease, Major." Menendez snagged a cola from the open six-pack. "Augur is an interesting individual. Did some good work during the war. Now it pays us to watch what he's watching, and letting him play his games is a small price to pay for that."

"Then you'd better tell your man not to get caught red-handed in my jurisdiction," said Captain Delrio. "Just because we're grateful to him at the moment doesn't mean he's got a permanent Get-Out-of-Jail-Free card."

"Augur is his own man, I'm afraid," said Menendez.

"I'll take care of passing along the warning," Boone told the captain. To Menendez, he said, "What about

Sergeant Birki—how badly is he going to get hit for his part in all this? If he needs somebody to testify on his behalf—“

Menendez smiled. “Birki is up for a Silver Star for his role in infiltrating an insurrectionist cell. So are you, for your actions, even though you'll never be able to let anyone read the citation or be able to wear the medal in public.”

“He can wear it on his pajamas.” Morovsky opened the pizza box and took out a slice of pepperoni and cheese. “At least, so long as he remembers to put his coat on before going out to pick up the newspaper in the morning.”

“Good thing I've got my friends to keep me humble,” Boone said. He reached out and took a slice of pizza for himself. “And I think we've finally cleared up the loose ends for this particular case.”

“Almost,” Delrio said. She turned back to her desk computer and pressed the printout button. “Someone besides the folk in this room seems to have found out about your service to humanity. You've just been requested by the very highest levels to be assigned to a special task, and the mayor's approved your posting.”

Boone regarded the printout in the captain's hand with suspicion. “Doing what?”

“You've been tapped to act as head of security when the North American Taelon Companion Da'an makes his first in-person public appearance, right here in Denver. Da'an will be sharing the stage with Jonathan Doors himself.”

Boone set the slice of pizza down untouched on Delrio's desk blotter. "Oh, no."

"Oh, yes," said Menendez. "You were in the service long enough to learn about the traditional reward for proving that you can walk on water—the next time around, they give you deeper water with bigger waves in it."

"I know, Colonel. I know." Boone gave a sigh of resignation. "When does this new job start?"

"Effective immediately," Delrio said.

"Effective in three hours, you mean," Boone said. "I need to go over the situation with my wife."

He pulled out his global and punched in Kate's code. "Honey, I'm going to be home early today," he said, then slid the screen shut again and turned back to Captain Delrio. "Better make that 'effective in four hours.' I don't believe in short conversations."

About the Authors

Debra Doyle and James D. Macdonald are the authors of the *Mageworlds* science-fiction adventure series, as well as young-adult fiction, and other works. They live in New Hampshire.